DOG TOWN is set on th(Sydney, Australia.

The story came to the author in a dream. A small dog named Harry, who loved to run, found himself lost in a strange town. Harry's best friend, Junior, was very sad about his disappearance. In this dream, the small dogs and big dogs lived apart, and cats were extinct. This formed the basis of Dog Town.

The Dog Paddle Challenge in Dog Town is based on a real race called the annual Scotland Island Dog Race. This event is a doggie-paddle race of 600 metres from Scotland Island to the ferry jetty at Church Point, in Sydney's northern beaches. The entry fee is a tin of dog food and the winning dog of each category takes all. There is only one rule: the owners must accompany their dog in the race, either by swimming, or on kayak or body-board, but the dogs must swim the race. And the dogs love it.

In 2019, a cat entered the race for the first time.

The author watched this race one year, and saw how much fun the dogs had. She simply had to include the race in this book.

DOG TOWN

DEBBIE L RICHARDSON

Dog Town

Written by Debbie L Richardson

Published by D L Richardson
www.dlrichardson.com

This book is a work of fiction. The names, characters, places, and incidents are fictitious or have been used fictitiously, and are not to be construed as real in any way. Any resemblance to persons, living or dead, actual events, locales, or organisations is entirely coincidental.

Copyright (c) 2020 Debbie L Richardson

Written using English (Australia) spelling

All Rights Are Reserved. No part of this book may be used or reproduced in any manner whatsoever without written permission, except in the case of brief quotations embodied in critical articles and reviews.

First print publication: April 1, 2020

CONTENTS

Chapter 1

HARRY'S ODD DREAM

HARRY was dreaming that a cat fell out of the sky and landed on his head.

He woke at once. Darkness filled his kennel; he couldn't be sure if it was very late or very early. Now wide awake, he puzzled about the cat in his dream.

Cats were unheard of in Dog Town. The way summers without mosquitoes were unheard of. Or non-fattening chocolate bars were unheard of.

Baffled, Harry shifted his thoughts to something else. Bones. Toys. Yet when he closed his eyes, images of cats swam across his mind. They beckoned to him, calling out to him for help.

Harry sat up. A shiver settled over him. As he struggled to grasp the meaning of this odd dream, he became convinced that it meant something horrible for dog-kind.

The blanket at his feet offered a good place to avoid thinking on his dream any further. He hid under the blanket, until the heat of the summer's night made it hot enough to cook a roast.

Harry pushed his nose outside his kennel. It was hot and humid, without a breath of wind. Vastly different to that afternoon when the wind's temper had set every door in the house banging.

Even though it was too hot inside his kennel, he didn't want to leave it. Outside in his backyard, shadows skipped across the treetops. Shadows that didn't belong there, shouldn't be there without the wind or clouds to drive them.

"Just more of my bad dream," Harry whispered.

He retreated into his blanket and closed his eyes to go back to sleep.

It wasn't long before his bladder woke him up by announcing with a pinch in his belly that it wanted to be taken outside.

"Traitor," he growled at his abdominal region.

Determined to stay in bed, he twisted and turned, trying to find a comfortable position. He squeezed his legs together, but the pressure became unbearable. As unwilling as he was to go out into the darkness, he knew he would have to oblige his bladder's demands for relief.

"It was just a dream," he woofed quietly.

He stepped out into the darkness, just as shadows danced along the fence. They reminded him of the cat in his dream.

It had been a black cat with yellow eyes.

It knew Harry's name.

In Harry's dream, he and the cat had played together. They had laughed and rolled down grassy hills and tossed dandelions at each other. Then it had begun to drizzle with rain, and the cat had shown Harry a tunnel where he could stay dry.

This was all preposterously unbelievable,

of course. Harry had never played with a cat before. Harry had never even *met* a cat.

No dog had. Well, perhaps Old Roger had. Old Roger was the oldest small dog alive. But Old Roger never spoke about cats. No dog did. And there was good reason for this.

Cats were extinct.

Chapter 2

LET SLEEPING DOGS LIE

HARRY wasn't afraid of the dark – the bad dream had caused the flurry of worry inside him. But he *was* afraid of dew on the grass. He considered anything 'wet' to be harmful to his health.

Not only did Harry dislike dew, it made it impossible to sniff out a good potty spot. He weaved up and down the path, backing over his trail several times. Finally, unable to force himself to step out onto the damp lawn, he lifted his leg on the pole of the clothesline.

Just then a frog croaked, startling the dog. And because he was standing on three legs he almost toppled over.

"It's my imagination playing tricks on me," Harry said, with more bravado than he felt.

He bounded toward the house.

For the rest of the night, sleep teased Harry the way a gooey chocolate cake teased someone on a diet. He became afraid to close his eyes, because each time he did, he saw cats in the hundreds. They were everywhere, tumbling down from the sky, flying toward him. And each one hit him square on the head. He wouldn't have been at all surprised to wake up the next morning covered in bruises.

For the next hour he tossed and turned. Finally, when it seemed he'd be awake until dawn, he closed his eyes and the sleep fairies whisked him off to the land of nod.

Harry jolted awake moments later.

"Drats to cats," he said.

What on earth could it mean to be plagued by visions of cats?

While he had no clue what the dreams meant, he knew a dog that might.

Whenever Harry needed to hear the voice of reason, it spoke through his best friend, Junior. Junior was a Beagle. He had a white fur coat with brown spots. One of these spots sat over his eye to make it appear as if he wore a monocle.

Junior was the wisest dog Harry knew.

Harry braved the shadows once more. When he reached the clothesline, he stopped to stare at the gardenia bush that spread its branches guardedly along the fence. Normally, Harry communicated with his friend by way of a gap in the fence, usually concealed by the bush. Now, dew dampened the ground between the dog and the fence, sending a shiver of dread along Harry's spine.

He called out to his friend in a soft bark.

Nothing. Not a sound.

Harry willed his friend awake using the power of his mind, until he realised that his mind powers were another figment of his imagination.

"Come on, Junior," Harry cried out, louder this time. "Wake up. I need some of your good sense."

Harry detected movement, and this lifted

his mood. But the sound turned out to be a gush of wind teasing the gardenia bush awake.

Junior would never have believed me anyway, Harry thought.

But he knew someone else who might.

With a whoop of delight, Harry ran to the other side of the concrete path under the clothesline. Here, the fence was a hodge-podge of chicken wire and steel garden stakes, a result of a gale wind blowing the fence down a few months ago. This temporary fence allowed Harry a clear view of the neighbour's yard, all from the safety of the path. Although he suspected Fleabag – his other best friend – would also be fast asleep.

"Fleabag." Harry used a gentler tone, hoping his sing-song voice would carry across the yard and into her ear. "Are you awake?"

Fleabag was a Chihuahua with a shiny caramel-coloured coat. Like Junior, she was Harry's best friend. Unlike Junior – who would label Harry's dream an ominous warning – Fleabag was as bouncy as the ribbons on her collar. She was the type of dog who always found the positive in things. *She* would think Harry's dream was a wonderful foretelling.

But a foretelling of what? he wondered with a scowl. He would never find out what either dog thought if they could not be coaxed from their sleep.

"I do wish you would wake up," Harry said of his peacefully sleeping friends. Then he let out a series of hushed barks. "Wish, wish, wish."

Wishing out loud was dangerous. It increased his chances of spending the remainder of the night inside the laundry room. So he gave up wishing and returned to his kennel.

Counting the slats in the roof seemed like a good way to pass time, until he remembered that dogs lacked the ability to count. Instead, he squeezed his eyes shut and waited for the sleep fairies to whisk him back to the land of sleep.

They took their time.

When sleep finally arrived, it came for good. Harry slept uninterrupted for the remainder of the night.

In the morning, the dream lingered in the corners of his mind. He knew of only one way to chase this dream away.

He would hold a race around the streets of Dog Town.

Chapter 3

A RACE TO THE BEGINNING

DOG TOWN consists of two suburbs – Big Rover and Little Rover. Big dogs live in Big Rover. And small dogs live in Little Rover. This is Dog Law.

Big Rover lies in the north of Dog Town, and Little Rover lies in the south. Little Rover is relatively flat with approximately fifty single-storey and double-storey homes spread evenly across the township. It has a few nice shops to the north of town, near a lovely park. In this park is a giant brick tower with a clock halfway up its south-facing wall.

Where Little Rover is a place alive with activity, Big Rover is a place where things go to rest. It has fewer houses and about twenty mansion-styled homes that are built on very large blocks. It has dozens of sheds that could store aeroplanes. Large treeless plots of dirty land are filled to the brim with garden and household stuff. At its northernmost end there is a steep hill leading to a wild forest, however this forest is uninhabited by man or beast.

A wooden fence runs east to west along the border of Little Rover and Big Rover, as a constant reminder to the inhabitants of Dog Town that they do not get along.

A large body of water sits to the west of both towns. This body of water, known as Buster Bay, is the only thing the two precincts share, although on a strict roster.

On the shoreline of Buster Bay, smack bang in the middle of Dog Town, there is an unpainted wooden jetty. It operates a ferry service to an island inhabited by Furless Ones. This island is known as Mystery Island because it is a mystery to the dogs how the island stays there without floating away.

Once a year, when the nights are so hot that it seems the wind has run out of puff, a group of dogs from Big Rover board a ferry bound for Mystery Island. These dogs then compete in a race across the water. They start the race at Mystery Island and end at the jetty on Buster Bay's shore. This race is known as the Dog Paddle Challenge.

The dogs of Little Rover are forbidden from participating in this race. This, again, is Dog Law. This ban, however, does not deter the small dogs from holding their own race. On a regular basis they run around the streets of Little Rover, starting at the abandoned shops on Sit Boy Lane. The race ends at the clock tower on Good Girl Avenue.

Such a street race was currently underway.

***

HARRY spied the bell of the clock tower over the treetops. He heard the bell strike the first of twelve chimes.

"First place, here I come," he whooped with delight.

"First to the finish line has to take a bath," Fleabag shouted, right on his tail.

"Stop changing the rules, Fleabag," he barked.

"At least we can tolerate a bath," Junior cried out, though from further away.

Junior was talking about Harry's phobia – called ablutophobia, a fear of water. Harry suffered terribly from it. He was afraid to get too close to his water bowl in case it tipped over. And he never bathed. His brown coat could very well have been white underneath the dirt for all anyone knew.

He could see no point in bathing anyway, because he often rolled in something filthy afterwards.

Even now, the thought of water made Harry look up at the sky. Above, he saw a wide expanse of blue and not a cloud in sight. Just the way he liked it.

Sneaking a look behind him, he noticed Junior trailing behind in third place. As usual, Junior's attention was on the traffic rather than on the race. But Fleabag, who was in second place, was gaining on him. She was competitive, probably more competitive than Harry, yet something other than canine competitiveness propelled Harry forward.

Harry was the champion racer, and he'd been the champion racer for two years. He wasn't about to quit and give up the title and the prestige that came with it. (Did he mention that the fastest dog also got a share of all Little Rover's bones?)

The small dogs of Little Rover looked up to the fastest dog, and Harry quite simple adored the adoration that came from being a champion.

He dug his nails into the asphalt and did a sideways slide out of Fifi Street. As he swerved into Good Girl Avenue, he narrowly avoided a collision with a bicycle carrying a young Furless One.

"Watch out, Harry!" Fleabag yapped.

Harry ducked. The bike pedal came within an inch of his head.

"I swear they act like they own the roads," he mumbled.

He dug his nails into the asphalt and quickly regained the distance he'd lost during his near collision with the bike.

When Harry next looked over his

shoulder, he saw that Junior was overtaking Fleabag. He lowered his head and charged toward the finish line, where a bright yellow banner swung in the air between two streetlights on Good Girl Avenue.

As the banner came into sight, Harry bit down on the pain that snaked up his legs. He told his feet to go faster, and they obeyed. Anyone looking would have seen his ears pressed flat against his head and his eyes squeezed into narrow slits. (This was to stop the bugs from crashing into his eyeballs).

And then, when his heart felt like it would explode, the race was over. Harry had won.

The other racers congratulated him, marvelling at how such a small dog could run so fast. Harry often wondered about this too. He was a dog of mixed-breeding and unknown origin. A pound puppy to be precise. Nothing special about Harry at all. Except that he was as fast as a deer and as zippy as a blowfly.

After the street race, some of the small dogs went home to rest. But some of the dogs went home to prepare, because the *real* race had yet to be run. That race would take place later that night.

Chapter 4

A DEATH WISH

JUNIOR had excellent night vision. A fact he did not like because it made it easier to *see* trouble at night.

It was now later that night, and six pint-sized lapdogs marched toward Stumpy Tail Square for a special kind of race. Junior didn't like these night races, but if Harry was going, someone had to keep him out of trouble.

Harry led the way. Junior followed next in line. Then Fleabag and three other small dogs named Pablo, Kevin, and Teena.

Marching toward the secret entrance into Big Rover was a foolhardy mission. (These dogs had the combined martial art skills of an Olympic papier mâché champion). Yet they marched anyway.

Fleabag appeared at Junior's side. "Hey, I almost beat you today," she said with a grin.

"You let me win, Fleabag," Junior said. "It's better to lose fairly than to win unfairly."

"As if I'd *let* you win. I broke a nail at the last turn."

Junior glanced behind him. The shadows appeared darker tonight.

"I have an awful feeling," he said. "I just want to make my concerns known now, in case something bad happens and I have to say 'I told you so'."

Fleabag rolled her eyes. "You always have a bad feeling. For example, you said we'd get sick if we ate that dead fish on the beach."

"It was smelly and rotten—"

"Then you said we'd get worms if we ate dirt."

"I stand by that claim."

"And then you said we'd choke on the

teddy bear's eyes."

"What are you trying to say, Fleabag? That I worry too much?"

"You're more cautious than a Boy Scout at a pedestrian crossing."

Junior felt his scowl deepen. "I'm serious, Fleabag. This sixth sense is worse than normal."

She sighed. "Everything is going to be fine. We're going to creep up on the big dogs and yell 'boo' at them, just like we do every week. You do realise, my good friend, that by never kicking up your heels, you'll wind up kicking yourself later."

"Wow, Fleabag. That was profound."

She poked her tongue out at him. "That's what I get from hanging around you too much. Now come on, the others are waiting on us."

The others were at a place known as Stumpy Tail Square. It was a grassy area with wooden tables and chairs, popular with the Furless Ones for picnics and barbeques.

A sign stood near the main road banning all dogs from the area. None of the dogs had developed the skills that made reading possible. They knew of this ban from walks with their Furless Ones who would point at the sign as the dogs tugged at the lead to chase down the scent of a sausage.

They were here, not in defiance of the Furless Ones' laws, but because Stumpy Tail Square backed onto the border that separated Little Rover and Big Rover.

The dogs met at this spot before and after a night race, accessing Big Rover through a hole in the fence.

Junior could recall the exact day his best friend, Harry, had found the hole in the fence. It had been when the two of them were out chasing lizards. Since that day, Harry had been organising guided tours into Big Rover, and Junior had been urging him not to.

Fleabag had come up with a compromise. Harry could run these races, and Junior could impose some strict rules.

Such as: numbers on these outings were strictly limited; most dogs had to book days in advance; and bookings were essential.

Six small dogs were now lingering around a small Bottlebrush plant. Some of them licked the nectar off the dropped flowers because they were sugary-sweet. These dogs never got treats at home. Some dogs sniffed around the tables hoping to find stray pieces of sausage. Some wished they had stayed at home. Yet all waited with bated breath for Harry to give them 'the signal'.

Harry pulled his head back though the gap in the fence. He lifted a paw.

"The coast is clear," he said with glee. "The big dogs are nowhere in sight."

"Marvellous news," Junior said in a dull tone. "Because I would hate to cancel."

"You know there's only one reason to cancel," Harry said. "And there is not a raindrop in sight."

Harry turned and addressed the gathered dogs. "Step right up and be prepared to be scared. Vet surgeries are less terrifying than where you are about to enter. Even your neighbour's front lawn is less foreboding than tonight's Tour of Terror."

The small dogs let out a combined gasp of fright.

"But wait, there's more," Harry continued. "Nothing in your wildest doggy dreams will prepare you for your own starring role in a little flick I like to call, Dog Eat Dog."

"Harry!" Fleabag scolded. "You're

spooking the pup."

The pup she referred to, Pablo, was an ochre-coloured Pomeranian on his first trip into Big Rover. An already fluffy dog, the nearer Pablo got to the big dogs the more he puffed up. He now resembled a twelve-inch pompom.

"He's making it up," Fleabag told Pablo. "It's perfectly safe inside Big Rover."

"Sure it is," Harry said. "And to prove it I'll go first."

Junior held his breath as he watched Harry disappear through the hole.

Then a paw waved at them to follow.

The remaining dogs had little choice but to abide by their code of loyalty and follow him through. Junior led the way as they hurried toward the rendezvous point which was a truck tyre.

It was dark and a little crowded inside the tyre. (If anyone is interested to know how many lapdogs can be squeezed inside a truck tyre, the answer is six.) Huddled together, the dogs started shaking, some with excitement, most with fear.

Teena, a Welsh Corgi, said nervously, "This is my second time in Big Rover. I'm not sure if I'm scared or excited. I'll think I'll let you know tomorrow."

Her little brother, Pablo, piped up and said, "Oh, I know I'm scared."

"Someone's fur is tickling my nose," Kevin said. He was a French Bulldog who was another first timer to Big Rover, having been given the booking as a birthday present. "Has anyone bathed in lavender? That scent plays havoc with my nose hairs."

"Quiet, everyone," Harry whispered. "It's best if the big dogs are taken by surprise."

The big dogs Junior wanted Harry to avoid waking prematurely were at the far end of Big Rover. They were secured on chains inside six-foot-square steel reinforced enclosures. They ate once a day, and by Junior's calculations they had last eaten three hours ago, right at dusk. But dogs are dogs and will force food into a full belly if necessary.

"I've changed my mind," Pablo said, giving Junior a wide-eyed stare. "Harry said this would be fun. Being eaten by a big dog is hardly what I'd call fun. I'd like to go home now."

"Too late, Pablo," Teena said. "I'm staying and you're coming."

Pablo sighed heavily. Dog Law declared that he had to do whatever his big sister told him to do.

Junior put a comforting paw on Pablo's shoulder.

"You'll be okay, mate," he said.

"But I thought we were only going as far as the border," Pablo mumbled.

"You've waited so long for this," Harry said. "Trust me, Pablo. Nothing is going to happen to you."

"You'll be fine," Teena added. "Just stick close by my side, and when the times comes, run like the vet's got a needle in her hand."

"That's the most important rule," Junior said in earnest. "Everyone, stick together. No wandering off."

"And let Harry, Junior, and I stay out in front," Fleabag added. "We've had more experience at this."

Harry had a big grin on his face. "When the big dogs strike – and strike they will – stay close beside your buddy."

Junior allocated the dogs into teams of two. He teamed himself up with Pablo.

"Is everyone ready?" Fleabag asked.

By entering Big Rover, the dogs were in direct violation of Dog Law. Junior felt the need to remind Harry of this.

"Why are we forcing Pablo to come with us if he'd rather go home?" Junior asked Harry. "We're already breaking Dog Law. Must we add abduction to our list of crimes?"

Harry gave Junior a knowing smile. "The big dogs are well secured inside their pens."

"Where they're meant to be," Junior said. "Instead of breaking a good number of Dog Laws like we are."

Harry flicked Junior a look of annoyance. "You're killing my vibe, brother. Come on."

Then Harry jumped out of the tyre.

Arguing with Harry was about as unproductive as barking at a garden gnome, Junior realised.

In a matter of seconds, the dogs bailed out of the truck tyre. Then they took the same route as was their habit – Harry way out in front as though he was pulling on an invisible leash while the rest followed with the cheerlessness of dogs forced to wear silly hats.

Cautiously, they headed north along Princess Avenue, where they resisted the urge to wee on old sofas. Then they turned right onto Here Boy Road, a place where fruit went to die by the glorious smell of it. They stopped for a moment when they reached the T-intersection.

At this junction, a metal sign leaned to the right. Like the sign at Stumpy Tail Square, this one had strange letterings that were indecipherable to the dogs.

They did not need to understand the strange markings to know if they went left they'd be on Rusty Street. More importantly, this intersection signalled the point of no return.

Rusty Street led the dogs to Barks A Lot Boulevard. One street away from where the big dogs lived.

The small dogs headed along Rusty Street. Junior, however, hung back. He stood staring up at the sign as though expecting it to tell him something. If any dog could understand a foreign language, it would be Junior. But the sign gave him no hints about why his nerves were rattled.

Fleabag appeared at Junior's side, startling him. He shuddered, because if she could sneak up on him, so could a big dog.

"No wandering off," Fleabag said. "We're supposed to stick to the buddy system. Your rules, remember?"

With a heavy sigh, Junior re-joined the line. He gave his buddy, Pablo, a forced smile.

"Pay no attention to me," Junior told the pup. "I'm more cautious than a canary in an underground mine."

"Oh, I'm a bit excited now that we've crossed into Big Rover," Pablo said, his wide-eyed look belying his courageous words.

"It's all about having fun," Fleabag said from behind. "And you know what? I'll bet those big dogs are actually soft and sweet on the inside."

"I beg to differ," Junior scoffed. "They're mean and vicious. Mark my words. They'll eat us one of these days."

"I doubt that. Hasn't it ever struck you as odd that we always manage to get away unharmed?"

Junior titled his head. "What are you saying? That the big dogs *let* us escape?"

"Come on now," Harry said from the front of the line. "You know we always escape because the big dogs are stupid. It takes their huge heads half the night to figure out how to unbuckle their collars."

This gave all the dogs a chuckle. All except Junior.

"Quit being so negative, will you?" Fleabag told him harshly.

"Sorry. I just have a bad feeling."

Her tone softened. "Look on the bright side, Junior. The sooner you get this over and done with, the sooner you can go home and curl up in your basket. So relax, will ya."

But Junior would never be able to relax.

Not while the scent of big dogs hung in the air.

Chapter 5

CAUGHT OFF GUARD

JUNIOR felt a sudden drop in temperature. Though it could have been frightful shivers running up and down his spine. It was quiet in Big Rover. Too quiet. The troop walked with care and purpose. If they were to accidentally knock into any of the countless bits and pieces that were strewn all over the road, it would be all over for them.

And yet, they continued to march without incident.

The big dogs must be fast asleep, Junior thought.

Not a sound could be heard except for the distant chirps of crickets and the faraway croaks of frogs. The small dogs listened with their super canine hearing for any sign of activity. Their noses were on high alert for the smell of big dogs.

It was a cloudless night. The moon beamed bright silver rays, lighting the path forward. It glinted off the metal window frames and hubcaps lying all over the place.

But the dogs didn't need the moonlight to see by. They all possessed exceptional night vision.

Not that it would have made much difference, Junior reminded himself. Big dogs had exceptional night vision too, and any one of them could be out of their pen and spying on them.

The feeling that Junior was being watched made his paws start to sweat. He didn't like being in Big Rover.

Moments after turning right onto Barks A Lot Boulevard, a powerful smell halted Junior in his tracks.

"What's that?" Junior asked.

"Hold up," Harry said from up front.

He held his paw in a stop signal. Then he began to sniff the ground.

The other dogs began sniffing the ground.

"It's a giant dog poo," Junior gasped, horror-struck. His hackles stood on their ends. "And it looks fresh."

The others jumped about in a state of worry, yet Harry seemed unperturbed. He continued sniffing the poo.

"There's a familiarity about this," he said. "I just can't quite place my paw on it."

"It must be déjá poo," Fleabag said, giggling.

Junior's nose twitched. "We should turn back. Now!"

He turned to face home but was stopped in his tracks by a voice that boomed as loud as a cannon.

"What do you think you trespassing troublemakers are doing?"

The voice was instantly recognisable to the small dogs. It belonged to Grizzly, the leader of Big Rover. He was a Doberman Pinscher with a coat as dark as a black bear, and he had the temper to match.

"Well, well, well," Grizzly growled. "What have we here? The petite pooch parade is out for a moonlit stroll. How utterly adorable."

The small dogs began to quiver. And then, like spent battery-powered toys they lost all use of motion and became still. Frozen to the ground and unable to move their feet, it was as though they were hoping to develop the ability to become invisible at will.

To Junior's great dismay, this didn't happen.

"And to what do I owe the pleasure of your presence in Big Rover?" Grizzly asked.

Grizzly's joy was evident in the way he sized them up. He eyed them with greed, like a treat was hidden inside one of the dogs and he had to guess which one. He ran his pink tongue over his glistening teeth.

Just when Junior had given up all hope of getting out of Big Rover alive, Grizzly twisted his head and stared off in another direction. His ears twitched as fast as his nose. While he was distracted, the small dogs glanced at one another.

Maybe they were being given a lucky

break, Junior thought.

But Grizzly's averted attention quickly returned to the intruders.

"Not that I'm opposed to home delivered meals," Grizzly said, his full attention on the intruders. "I mean free food is free food, but what *are* you walking snacks doing in Big Rover?"

The small dogs stood as rock-solid as garden gnomes. Not only had they lost the ability to move, it seemed they had lost the power of speech too.

Grizzly circled the small dogs. "What shall I call this menu selection? Perhaps I'll call you Pets on Baguettes." Then he said in a loud voice, over his shoulder, "What do you reckon boys?"

Two shapes stepped out from the shadows and stood beside Grizzly – Diesel, a German Shepherd, and Chain, a Rottweiler. They were Grizzly's henchdogs. Neither was as clever as Grizzly, but both were equally as mean-spirited.

The small dogs still could not move.

"I see a buffet of Pluto Pups," Diesel said.

"I see Meals on Wheels." This from Chain.

Diesel gave Chain the evil eye. "How can they be Meals on Wheels if they've got paws for feet?"

"I'll give them each a skateboard."

"Will you two keep quiet," Grizzly said.

He walked up to Harry who was at the front of the line and sniffed at the small dog's head. Then he leaned down and looked deep into Harry's eyes. Whatever he saw, it made him smile wickedly. Then he swept his piercing brown eyes over the rest of the trespassers. Back and forth his probing gaze went.

And still the small dogs did not move.

Diesel growled. "What do you say we give these mutts to the count of three to scram on outa here before we arrest them, boss."

"I like those odds," Chain said, licking his lips.

Grizzly nodded in agreement. "What do we do with trespassers, boys?"

"We eat trespassers, boss," Diesel said.

"And trespassers that survive that, will be eaten again," Chain added.

Grizzly pulled his lips into a menacing grin. When he growled, it rumbled like thunder, making his teeth vibrate.

He took a step toward the small dogs. First one paw. Then the other. The small dogs stood so rock-solid they could have supported a bridge.

"You are supposed to flee in a mad panic," Grizzly said, with a deep scowl. "I'm about to crush your necks with my powerful jaws."

Junior was too terrified to move.

This was the first time that the small dogs had run into the big dogs at night in their own territory. Like Fleabag had said earlier, the big dogs were *always* in their pens. What were they doing out of them?

Grizzly lowered his head. "Forget counting to three," he said. "Let's get 'em, boys."

The big dogs lunged, exposing pointy teeth that shone like slivers of steel. The attacking dogs barked like rabid animals, spraying drool and spittle everywhere.

The bad thing that Junior had predicted would happen was happening.

The small dogs were under attack.

Chapter 6

IN THE RUNNING

HARRY snapped himself out of the trance.

"Run!" he yelled, and every dog did exactly that.

But they took off in a disorderly fashion, like a handful of wound-up toys had been released onto a slippery surface.

Kevin started running first, but he became caught up in chasing his tail. He twirled and twirled, creating a mini tornado.

Teena barked so violently she propelled

herself backwards. She only managed to stop when she bumped up against a six-foot-high stack of hubcaps. The metal discs came hurtling toward the dogs at an alarming speed.

Harry saw Teena jump out of the way. Then she reached for Pablo's collar. She tugged and tugged, but her brother's feet might as well have been concreted to the ground.

"Pablo!" Harry urged. He cried out again, more urgently this time. "Pablo! Run!"

Pablo stared at the big dogs as though he was hypnotised.

"Pablo!" Teena cried, pulling harder on his collar.

By now, Kevin's mini tornado had taken on a life of its own. Wispy tendrils clutched madly at anything in reach, but they grasped only air. Seemingly angered by this, the vortex pulled itself into the shape of a bowling ball and made a beeline for Pablo and Teena.

About to become swept up into the swirling vortex, Teena let rip one final demanding bark that was likely to have caused a fur ball to be coughed up.

"Pablo! Move your butt!"

At last, her brother came to his senses and

jumped high into the air,

Only to jump straight into the clutches of a big dog.

Chain held Pablo by the scruff of his neck, and poor Teena was left hanging off Pablo's collar. The humidity of the night must have made Chain's paw clammy, because Harry watched as Pablo slid out of Chain's grasp and fell to the ground.

Teena jumped deftly out of the way, but Pablo had passed out cold mid-flight.

Harry ran to the small dog. "Pablo. Wake up!"

Pablo's blackout was momentary. The small dog leapt up and chased after his sister, running so fast that his barks were heard long afterwards.

"Fleabag!" Junior yelled at Harry's side. "Get out of here,"

"You go," she shouted. "I'll hold them off."

Perhaps in a previous life Fleabag had been a Sheep Dog, Harry thought, as he watched her snap at the heels of the big dogs. A starving mosquito at a barefoot convention would have been less tenacious. Fleabag darted from ankle to ankle, relentless in her pursuit to bring down the big dogs.

Until Grizzly seized her by the scruff of her neck and flung her into a nearby garbage bin.

She yelped, but she was not knocked out.

"Scram, Fleabag," Grizzly growled. "Get outa here before I get *real* cranky."

Fleabag turned toward home. Harry was still trying to escape the jaws of the other two big dogs.

As Junior and Fleabag sped past him, they knocked Harry sideways. He hit his head on the metal trashcan.

Darkness clawed at his eyelids.

Everything went black.

***

GRIZZLY watched the small dogs flee for their lives.

It almost put a smile on his face.

Their frightened barks could be heard in the far-off distance. After a few minutes they began to die down until it was quiet once again. Except for the distant sound of croaking frogs, chirping crickets, and the soft hum given off by the porch lights that had come on when the commotion had started.

"Well, that was a pleasant intermission," Grizzly said with a chuckle. "But we've got work to do. It's around here some place, boys. And we have to find it."

"We've already looked everywhere, boss. Are you sure it's here?" Diesel asked.

"Are you calling me a liar? Or are you calling me delusional? What exactly is it you're saying?"

"I'm not saying either, boss. All I'm saying is we've looked everywhere. The place is too well hidden."

"No, Diesel," Grizzly said, raising his snout to sniff the air. "Our problem is that we're not thinking like them."

He was, of course, talking about cats.

Chapter 7

A TUNNEL IS FOUND

HARRY was sent sailing through the air after Fleabag bumped into him. He had landed headfirst and been knocked out cold. Yet in contrast to Pablo, who had come to instantly, Harry had remained unconscious. When he'd finally woken up, he had a sore head and sore backside from being firmly wedged between two large dumpsters.

Not sure how long he'd been out cold for, it was at least peaceful. This was a far cry from the chaotic noise when the big dogs had ambushed them earlier.

"Junior? Fleabag?" Harry said softly.

Instead of getting an answer, he was treated to a symphony of banging and crashing. From the sounds of it, Grizzly, Diesel, and Chain were still on the prowl.

"Will you stop bumping into everything?" a voice Harry recognized as Grizzly's barked. "You're making enough noise to wake the dead."

"I was never any good at playing hide and seek." (This from Chain.) "It's my big bones. They make sneaking around tight places a nightmare."

"Big boned!" a third voice (Diesel's) cried out. "You eat more than you weigh. Ever heard of eating in moderation?"

"How about we use our little voices?" Grizzly said. "Do you think you two can handle something as simple as whispering?"

Grizzly sounds peeved about something, Harry thought. He took the big dog's frustration as a sign that his friends had made it safely out of Big Rover. But why were they still on the prowl? he wondered.

Anxious to get home to check on his

friends, Harry wriggled his body along the dumpsters until he fell through to the other side. He landed on grass that was long and spindly. Wild grass was his favourite kind. It was always alive with bugs and lizards, and sometimes mice. When a frog hopped out of a covering of paspalum grass, Harry forgot all about looking for his friends and took off after it.

He followed the amphibian, wagging his tail with delight. When it bounced over a thicket of tall grass, Harry bounded after it. Together the frog and the dog bounded across the paddock. When the frog went "Cro-oak", Harry imagined that it said, "Give it your best shot, Harry, I bet I can hop better than you".

Invigorated by the challenge, Harry mimicked the frog as they hopped their way up a small embankment. Harry had become so preoccupied with his game of chase that he almost missed an unusual smell that floated on the breeze.

It was a scent unlike anything he'd ever come across before. He halted his chase after the frog, but just as quickly, the aroma was picked up by the breeze and carried away. It was as if it had never existed, so Harry readied himself to pounce after the frog.

This time, the wind made its presence known by ruffling a branch of wild ferns apart.

There, behind the ferns, Harry saw a hole in the hill. The frog was immediately forgotten about as Harry's hackles rose.

Not a hole, he told himself. But a tunnel.

Well, Harry was a bitza of a dog – a bit of this and a bit of that – which meant he could have been born to be anything. He could have been born to go into tunnels after rabbits and rats. He could have been born to round up sheep. There was no way of telling what he was meant to do unless he tried.

He stepped into the tunnel.

It was bigger than Harry and about as round as a soccer ball. Here at the entrance, the scent of animal droppings was much stronger. And it was from an animal Harry was unfamiliar with.

As well as the strange smells, unusual sounds rebounded from far within the tunnel. They sounded like the noises made at parties.

(Occasionally, parties were held by the Furless Ones at the house where Harry lived.

Although he was never invited and was always locked in the laundry. All because he'd once chewed a few shoes.)

Whoops and cheers and songs and applause danced along the walls of the tunnel. But what sort of odd creature would be having a party underground? Harry wondered.

Rabbits seemed like a possible culprit. But rabbits hated noise. It made them twitch all over.

Wombats also had tunnels like this one, but wombats were cranky fellows who would never allow their guests – if the anti-social creatures ever had any – to run rampant.

Whatever was at the end of the tunnel, it was intriguing.

Harry ran along the earthen floor, kicking up the dirt with his toenails. He sniffed at the air, hungry to eat up the exotic scents. He pushed his ears forward to vacuum up every sound. His tail beat from side to side in puppy delight. He could not remember when he had last been this excited.

Deep in thought, Harry didn't notice that the ground beneath his paws had changed from dirt to concrete until the clicking of his toenails on the ground began to echo. He slowed to a stop, worried that the noise might carry to the partygoers.

He took this moment to study his surroundings. They were dark, cool, and featureless. He saw a set of steps leading downwards. He glanced back the way he'd come. It was too late to go back. Wasn't it?

Stopping at the head of the stairs, he noticed that the noise and smell was intensified here. Ordinarily he was a dog who acted first, asked permission later. Now he hesitated, telling himself he needed to catch his breath. What really made him hesitate was an unsettling feeling in his stomach.

He could hear Junior's voice in his head, telling him about his bad feeling. Harry shook his body to rid himself of the silliness. He was letting his imagination run wild, that's all. There wasn't a big bad monster waiting for him.

He began his descent into the strange underground world.

Harry made it to the bottom unharmed. He found himself in a large underground room made entirely out of concrete. It had a concrete floor and concrete walls, and it was windowless, which made the air warm. It stank too, like week-old bread.

Ahead he saw an archway. Even a dog without an over-active imagination would have guessed that something daunting lurked on the other side.

Harry bit his tongue to stop the volley of yaps that kept threatening to give his presence away to the party-revellers. His hackles stood on end. This was scarier than being chased by the big dogs.

And still, he didn't turn back. Instead, he tiptoed closer to the doorway.

He rested his paws on the archway and lifting his body up high to get a good look at what lay on the other side.

What he saw had to be an hallucination.

"I must have hit my head pretty hard," he said. "Because, great dog biscuit. I've found Cat World."

Chapter 8

SPY GAMES

HARRY had seen cats in picture books but never in real life. What he'd seen in these books had not interested him. So indifferent was he, he could see why they'd become extinct. Still, despite being a dog with the imagination to conjure up a good story, even *he* had doubts whether he could have created a world as magical and psychedelic as the one he saw now.

Cat World was a fluffy sea of colour, with waves of chocolate-brown, gingers, and rusty-reds. There was fur as black as oil, and fur as white as snow. There were coats the colour of whipped cream and coats the colour of fudge. As well as sandy-beige and sooty-beige, and fur as grey as clouds both stormy and overcast.

Every corner, every nook and cranny, and every crevice contained a cat of a different colour.

And the patterns!

There were as many patterns as there were colours. Harry saw stripes on stripes, stripes along the ridge, spots on stripes, spots on spots.

There were blotches on heads and ears, and blotches on tails and paws. Indeed, many of the cats looked as if an artist had painted them blindfolded.

The pictures in the books had done little to convey other aspects of the cats. Like how the smells reminded Harry of rotting fish. And there was another pungent odour that he could not place, but it was similar to the eye-stinging, nose-tickling water that featured in many neighbourhood swimming pools. Even the air seemed to have a taste. It was dry and it stuck to the inside of his throat. Like peanut butter, he thought.

The sounds of Cat World were louder now that he was on top of them. And to a dog with exceptional hearing, the high-pitched shouting and squealing (for cats spoke in shrill voices) started to hurt his ears.

Pressing himself against the archway to make his body as flat as possible, Harry noticed dozens of mirrors. They were positioned around the walls at sloping angles. He suspected they were facing one another to reflect light. There were tapered flares emitting from the candles that sat in a puddle of melted wax in the centre of the room.

He stayed pressed against the archway and used the mirrors to spy on the cats. He should have felt awkward spying on them. Instead, he drooled over Cat World as he would a juicy steak.

Cat World was filled with noise, colour, smells, and high energy. And Harry was loving every bit of being down here amongst the cats.

In the nearest corner, on Harry's left, six cats sat around a table playing a game of cards.

"Cheat," one of them said.

"I did no such thing, Philippe," another said. "I merely made my own interpretations of the rules."

"Still, you have to pick up a card, Humphrey," a third cat said. "He called you a cheat."

"*You* pick up a card," Humphrey said. "I demand we start a new game."

"You do this every time you start losing," Philippe said, throwing his cards down on the table. "We have yet to finish a single game."

Harry stared longingly at the poker chips, seeing them as things to chew on. If Junior were here, he reflected, he'd say they were things to choke on.

This sudden thought made Harry think about his friends. He hoped they'd made it safely out of Big Rover.

A scene in the mirror caught his interest. In the far right, cats were doing back-flips, dancing to a symphony of saucepans being banged upon by wooden spoons. Neither dancer nor musician seemed to care that they were out of sync with one another. And the dancing cats jumped as erratically as popping corn, while the musicians seemed engrossed in their unique blend of irregular rhythm.

Turning his head, Harry saw a huddle of

cats crammed onto a tattered lounge chair that was situated in the centre of the room. The cats jumped up and cheered every few minutes, doing a Mexican wave it seemed. Yet when Harry craned his neck, he saw that they were watching a fishing show on a television.

Then a yell, like a war cry, startled Harry.

"En guarde," went the shout.

Two gingers cats whizzed past, close enough for Harry to touch their matted-with-sweat coats.

He felt each swipe of their sharp claws, he winced as they spat and hissed, and when they howled as though a door had caught their tails, Harry almost ran to their aid.

Wisdom prevailed, and Harry stayed hidden. He did not want their needle-like claws used on him.

Fighting was a sport the small dogs never engaged in, preferring to snuggle and chase leaves. When Harry turned, he saw two cats at a game that was more to his liking. One cat had a beige head and chocolate-brown body, and the other had the same colouring, but in the opposite direction. They stood four feet apart, flicking a ping-pong ball along the ground to each other. Back and forth. Back and forth. As though the white ball was a bomb and it had to be gotten rid of right away.

Harry was amazed at their level of concentration amidst such distraction. He was even more amazed at his restraint. With every fibre of his body, he wanted to play with the ping-pong ball.

He was spared from acting impulsively, thus revealing himself, when a cat with a long, white, fluffy coat switched on a karaoke machine. The music was lovely. The singing was horrid.

As the white cat squealed, a shiver went up and down Harry's spine, briefly lifting the enchanted spell to remind him that it was time to leave. But Harry wasn't ready to go. Cat World was captivating.

He watched until the cat's activities drove him mad with jealousy. And when Harry's patience could take no more, a bell sounded.

Immediately the cats jumped up, and one after another they launched themselves as daintily as ballerinas through a gigantic picture frame, devoid of a picture of course, that was hung midway up the wall.

Harry waited until the last tail had disappeared through the picture frame, then he took a step inside the great hall of Cat World.

He longed to bite the poker chips and throw the ping-pong ball high into the air. He itched to have a go at banging the saucepans. He wanted to touch everything.

Yet he was also afraid.

What if this was a mirage? What if he was still stuck between the dumpsters and this was another of his crazy dreams? How would he convince his friends that Cat World was real if he was not sure about it himself?

With no windows to allow the cat's odours to escape, Harry's eyes began to water. And rather than risk knocking into the furniture, he backed quietly out of the room. He had seen enough anyway to know that he was not hallucinating.

Cat World was real.

The question remained whether he could convince his friends he was telling the truth.

Chapter 9

OH WHERE, OH WHERE CAN HE BE?

FLEABAG woke at the crack of dawn and hurried out of her kennel to check on Harry and Junior. In the light of day, their attack seemed more embarrassing than anything else. Bracing herself against the "I told you so" she expected from Junior, she was a little disappointed to find him curled up fast asleep on his porch.

She called out to him, but Junior was as still as a rock.

"Huh," she said. "That's unlike Junior to

pass up on the chance to prove a point. At least Harry will be up and planning a way to strike back at Grizzly."

But when she looked inside Harry's kennel it was empty.

As Fleabag walked back home it started to rain. Just lightly, but Harry was so terrified of water, even a summer shower would have him quivering. But how a summer rain could frighten anyone, Fleabag had no idea. They were as gentle as a sprinkler in the park.

Nevertheless, if Harry was lying seriously injured somewhere, he'd be petrified right now.

Fleabag roused Junior from his sleep by dragging his bed off the porch and onto the back lawn.

"We have to find Harry," she told him.

"Finding Harry means going back into Big Rover," Junior said, plucking tufts of grass out of his basket.

"So what are we waiting for?"

"Big Rover is too dangerous. You know the only reason we go is because Harry makes us."

"Pff," she said. "Harry doesn't *make* us. We choose to go because it's fun." She began pacing in the backyard. "We could go by ourselves. We owe it to Harry to at least look."

Junior shook his head. "Harry will be safely hidden away until it stops raining. He'll come home eventually. Like he always does."

Fleabag folded her paws one over the other. "Harry would go looking for us."

Junior sighed. "I knew I had a bad feeling about last night. And it's still tying my stomach into knots."

Minutes later, Fleabag and Junior made it to the hole in the fence. Fleabag poked her head through, but she had to bribe Junior with a treat.

Big Rover was just as scary by day, Fleabag realised, but for a different reason. Where at night it was crawling with shadows, by day it was packed with Furless Ones who marched about moving objects from one place to another. Some things they moved by hand, but most of the hard work was done by machines with tusks like steel elephants.

"I suppose we should start by looking where we got ambushed last night," Junior said.

The pair made their way along Rusty Street. To the untrained eye, they looked like two happy-go-lucky dogs taking themselves out for a walk. In reality, their eyes and ears were wide open, intent on picking up any trace of Harry's unique never-been-washed scent.

"Harry!" Junior shouted to be heard over the clanging and banging of the machines. "Harry! Where are you?"

"Harry," Fleabag sang out, trying to disguise her bark so it didn't sound like a small dog's yappity-yap-yap.

"Big Rover looks very different by day," Fleabag said, chewing her lip. "What if we get lost?"

"The same rule applies whether we're breaking into Big Rover by day or by night," Junior said. "We will be okay as long as we stay together."

They weaved their way past every conceivable machine that banged and clanged and whistled and rattled. They called out until their voices were weak and raspy.

"I feel guilty for running off last night," Fleabag said. They had ducked under a wooden crate to hide from a passing machine. "I should have done more to stop those big dogs."

Junior gave her a sympathetic look. "The only way you could stop Grizzly would be to get lodged in his throat."

"Still, if I'd paid attention to your ominous warning, then last night's disaster would have been avoided. I'm sorry."

"That's all right, Fleabag. If you paid attention to every doom and gloom thing I said, you'd never leave your kennel."

At least my dear friend would be at home where he ought to be, she thought.

"Then again," Junior added, "I know a few bad luck stories about kennels that would have you terrified of ever going inside one again. Why do you think I sleep in a basket?"

When an hour had gone by without finding their friend, they had to agree that the recent downpour had washed away every scent of big and small dog, including Harry.

Yet Fleabag was more worried that Grizzly was hiding somewhere and waiting to ambush them again.

She scowled as she remembered last night. Grizzly had *never* ambushed them before. The predictability of nothing bad ever happening was the only reason the small dogs continued to break into Big Rover. For Grizzly to do something out of habit was very un-doglike.

It was Grizzly's habit to stay inside his pen while the small dogs broke into Big Rover.

What were Grizzly, Diesel, and Chain doing sneaking around at night?

Fleabag sighed. "The only way we're going to know what happened is to go to the big dogs and ask them."

"What?" Junior backed up a step. "No way. We were lucky last night. We can't push our luck."

"They may have Harry locked up in their pens."

"And if they do? How are we supposed to break him out?"

"We'll figure that out when we get there."

Fleabag and Junior headed toward the concrete pen that was the formidable hub of Big Rover. If Harry had been captured, he'd probably be tied up inside one of the large steel-mesh kennels.

But when Junior and Fleabag got to the pens, they were empty.

Chapter 10

BAD TIDINGS

HARRY paused at the doorway of Cat World. His eyes searched for a memento to take back as proof that Cat World was real and not something he'd dreamed up. Ideally it had to be something he could carry in his paw, because dogs quite often left home without luggage.

There were many things that could fit inside his paw. The ping-pong ball, for example. But taking that would prove nothing. There were dozens of them in Little Rover.

The microphone was another example. And while taking that would prove nothing, it would save future generations from having to listen to the talentless cat who thought he was a pop star.

Harry finally found what he wanted to take back as proof. It was a substance like grains of sand, only with the pungent scent of cats. It was the best proof he had.

He turned to head for home. And it was then that he saw the statue. Towering high into the chamber, almost touching the ceiling.

"Great biscuit. It's a statue of a cat!"

Harry almost dropped his treasure. The gigantic statue glimmered like a ghost. It cast an eerie light that was as alive as the candles flickering in the middle of the room.

The statue beckoned Harry to come closer.

He crept toward it.

At first glance the stony surface appeared to be moving. It glistened the way water trickling down a stalagmite glistened.

When Harry was only a foot away, the materials of the statue became recognizable. It sent a quiver along his back.

He stepped in closer, both desperate and

afraid to confirm the materials of the statue.

Yet after one sniff, Harry knew.

The statue was made of puppy teeth!

His stomach twisted into an angry knot. His blood turned icy-cold. The hairs along his back and neck stood on their ends, almost pulling their roots out.

Harry turned and fled. He ran along the tunnel, gagging on the stale air that had suddenly become thick with the stench of deception. He ran and he kept on running until he burst through the ferns that concealed the tunnel's entrance.

Once outside, he began to cry.

Chapter 11

A TWIST IN THE TAIL

HARRY sat in the tunnel's entrance waiting for the sun shower to pass. He longed to rush home to the loveliness of Little Rover.

Little Rover is a happy place for a small dog to live. It is a town filled with feather Doonas on spacious beds. Good food can be gotten with a sad look. It has big yards for small dogs to chase lizards all day. There are long streets for long walks. (Although a big dog might argue that the yards in Little Rover were too small and the streets too short.)

In Little Rover there is always an adoring smile and a loving cuddle to be had. Young Furless Ones bounce with joy at the sight of a small dog. So too do elderly Furless Ones. And a small dog can spend all day sleeping on a lap without feeling the least bit like they're dodging responsibility.

Harry simply loved being a small dog. But when he'd recognised the stuff the statue was made from, he wished he was a dog with teeth the size of a machete.

Those thousands of pieces of tiny enamel had once belonged to the dogs of Dog Town. And now that Harry was free of Cat World's intoxicating allure, he wanted to go back and smash the statue to pieces.

He wanted to make the cats pay for stealing their teeth.

Above all, he wanted to punish them for making their teeth into an insulting effigy of a cat!

Harry's anger began to subside as he waited in the tunnel's entrance. It shifted from anger to denial until it finally settled on curiosity.

What on earth were the cats doing with the puppy teeth?

***

ANASTASIA had been hiding amongst a stack of wood at the bottom of the embankment that led to the secret tunnel, dreaming about lazing in a window, when she noticed a small dog sitting in the tunnel's entrance.

What is he doing here? she wondered

Anastasia was a black cat with yellow eyes who preferred to be on the surface at night where she was less likely to be seen. Yet her black coat blended perfectly with the dark knots of the old timber boat shed where she spied on the dog.

The more she watched, the more her curiosity grew. His name was Harry. She had often seen him racing around the streets. Usually he wore a stupid grin on his face, but today he looked miserable.

Anastasia was a gentle cat. She wanted to brush her cheek against his and ask him why he looked so sad.

And then it dawned on her. Harry must

have been in Cat World. He must have seen the statue.

She waited to make sure Harry didn't return with any other dogs. She waited until the sun was about to set and decided he was not going to return. Not today anyway.

It was only a matter of time before the dogs came.

She took off down the tunnel. The cats had to be warned of the impending disaster.

Chapter 12

STILL SEARCHING

JUNIOR followed Fleabag in search of Harry. They were at the big dog kennels, but they'd found nothing.

Grizzly surprised Junior when he popped out from underneath a pile of old clothes.

"Are you pups still meddling in our town?" Grizzly snapped. "I thought you'd have gotten the hint last night."

"We came to find our friend," Junior said, cranky and exhausted and in no mood for

Grizzly's temper. He had a fierce one of his own when he wanted. "Harry's been missing since last night."

"What do you want me to do about it?"

"We want you to return our friend to us."

Grizzly stuck his head underneath a mattress. Then he pulled it out.

"Go search somewhere else," Grizzly said with a growl. "And stay outa Big Rover while you're at it."

"What have you done with Harry?" Fleabag demanded.

Her loud yap startled Grizzly. He bumped into a trash can.

"I've done nothing with Harry," Grizzly barked. "I have no idea what you're talking about."

"Harry is missing," Fleabag cried.

"Not my concern right now."

Grizzly pushed his nose back under a pile of clothing and shook his head. Clothes were flung far and wide.

Grizzly was acting awfully strange, Junior thought. Big dogs usually threatened to eat small dogs at every opportunity. And this was about as good an opportunity as Grizzly was going to get.

"Harry's missing," Junior said, the serious tone causing Grizzly to stop doing whatever he was doing. "We believe you've captured him and you're holding him hostage."

"That's ridiculous," Grizzly barked. "Why would I hold him hostage? You've got nothing I want. Now scram on outa here before I break Dog Law and do something we'll both regret."

Junior stood his ground. "Not without Harry. Name your price, we'll give you what you want so long as you let him leave unharmed."

"Umm, let all of us leave unharmed," Fleabag added.

"Yes," Junior said. "We'll give you whatever you want. Just give us Harry and let us *all* leave unharmed."

Grizzly matched the stance of the small dogs, though he pulled off the tough dog look better than Junior and Fleabag.

"Beat it, will you," Grizzly growled. "Can't you see I'm busy."

"How dare you ignore us," Fleabag snapped. She darted out and nipped Grizzly on his hind leg.

Lightning quick, Grizzly whirled on

Fleabag. He pushed his nose right up into her face. He lifted his lips back in a sneer.

"Despite what you think," he said in a menacing tone, "big dogs have no need to take hostages. Now get out of Big Rover before I change my mind and tie you two up inside a pen with Chain. He's always looking for a snack."

"Grizzly, please help us," Junior begged. "Something's happened to Harry. Maybe you've seen him wandering around Big Rover."

"Maybe he hit his head," Fleabag added. Her voice began to quiver. "Maybe he's wandering around in a daze, unsure of who or where he is."

At last, Grizzly's attention was squarely on the small dogs. His brown eyes were hypnotic. Junior couldn't look away.

Then Grizzly's face broke out into a grin. "Seeing as how you put it nicely, I'll send out a patrol. When your little buddy is found he'll be sent home, unharmed. You have my word. Now get outa Big Rover and stop snooping around."

"You really haven't seen him?" Junior asked.

"I gave you my word, didn't I?"

Dog Word was always given truthfully. If

Grizzly was unaware of Harry's whereabouts, then Junior had to believe him. So where could Harry be? He and Fleabag had searched all over Little Rover and Big Rover and had not found a whiff of their best friend.

Grizzly glared at them until they were forced to leave. They stopped at Roll Over Road and ducked behind a trashcan. Junior poked his head out and noticed Grizzly giving a sneaky glimpse to the left and right, before he took off running down an alley.

"Do you think he's telling the truth?" Fleabag asked Junior. "Do you believe Harry's some place else, and not tied up like a pork chop ready to be eaten by Chain?"

Junior nodded. "We have no reason to doubt Grizzly. He gave his word. Still, he's acting very strange."

Junior indicated toward the distant figure of Grizzly, who had appeared out of the alley and was now jumping from rubbish pile to rubbish pile.

"Did you see the way he kept sniffing at the air?" Junior asked. "His nose twitched more than a rabbit's. If he isn't searching for Harry, then what is he searching for?"

Fleabag followed Junior's gaze. "He is a guard dog. It's in his nature to patrol."

Junior drew his brows together. "Actually, Fleabag, you said something last night that makes perfect sense now."

She scratched her head. "I said something sensible. Now I *know* I've been hanging around you too long."

"The big dogs are faster than us. Grizzly is the fastest dog of all, yet we always manage to outrun him. It's odd, don't you think?"

"What's odd is being told that it's a bad idea to lick smelly feet. But I get your point." She tilted her head. "Umm, what is your point?"

A machine came around the corner, surprising the dogs. They ducked beneath an overturned boat. Junior had to wait until the noisy machine drove by before he could speak again.

"This is my point, Fleabag," he said in a quiet voice. "Grizzly and his henchdogs could have eaten us for dinner last night. Even now, Grizzly could have eaten us. But he didn't."

Fleabag nodded. "Something is more important than eating us. But what?"

"I don't know. But Grizzly is definitely

searching for something that is *not* an ingredient in dog pie."

Fleabag gave Junior a sheepish smile. "Last night I might have said they are really soft and gentle on the inside, but I was only saying it to keep the mood light for the new dogs in the group. But you are the one who is right, Junior. We are lucky to be alive."

It was nice to hear Fleabag admit that Junior was right. But it didn't fix their immediate problem.

"One thing is for sure," Junior said. "They want us to stay out of Big Rover. But I'm not leaving without Harry."

Junior stuck his nose outside to see if any more machines were chugging down the street. They weren't. And yet he felt safer beneath the overturned boat. He might have stayed there for the rest of the day except their search through Big Rover would never be over until Harry was found.

"Come on," Junior said to Fleabag with a heavy sigh. "Grizzly can't be any madder at us than he already is. We might as well keep looking. We can't go home until we've found Harry."

Chapter 13

FOUND

JUNIOR and Fleabag called out for Harry until their throats were dry. And when Junior's legs threatened to fall off and his tired voice could yell no more, he dropped wearily to the ground.

"It's hopeless, Fleabag," Junior moaned. "There's no sign of Harry anywhere."

"Maybe he's made his way home," she suggested.

"I suppose. Come on then. Let's go home."

As the pair rounded the corner of Here

Boy Lane, a familiar face came running toward them. It was Harry.

"Junior! Fleabag!" Harry cried.

The missing dog was neither sporting a limp or bleeding from open wounds, so Junior guessed Harry had escaped being captured and tortured by the big dogs.

"Where the blazes have you been?" Junior barked crankily.

"We've been looking for you everywhere," added Fleabag in a happier tone.

Harry gave them both a big hug.

"You'll never believe where I've been," he said, jumping up and down in excitement.

"You had better not say you've been at home," Junior said.

Harry lowered his voice and flattened his ears. "No. It was marvellous. Absolutely marvellous. But it's too risky to talk here. We'll be overheard. Besides, I'm hungry. Let's eat."

Five minutes later the three dogs had satisfied their hunger with the food from Harry's bowl, plus a few scraps of bone he kept hidden in the backyard for emergencies.

Now, all three dogs were squeezed into Harry's kennel where they were safe from prying ears. Harry then related everything that had happened to him after the small dogs had fled last night's ambush by the big dogs.

"When I came around from being knocked out, everyone had gone," Harry said. "The big dogs were still prowling around. I knew I had to take another way home. I *thought* I knew every nook and cranny of Big Rover, but I found a secret tunnel."

Harry paused and stared at them. Junior could tell that Fleabag was enthralled with his tale. However, Junior was still to be convinced.

"Didn't you hear me?" Harry asked. "I found a secret tunnel."

"Ooooh," Fleabag said, wagging her tail.

"Let me guess," Junior said, in a disapproving tone. "You went into the tunnel."

Harry nodded. "I went into the tunnel."

"What did you find, Harry?" Fleabag asked.

Harry's eyes widened. "I found the lost city of Cat World."

Junior's face went hot with anger. "This is no time to display your weird sense of humour. We've been searching for you all morning. We're tired. And you have the nerve to sprout gibberish about Cat World. Every dog knows cats don't exist."

"I'm telling the truth." Harry's face wore a wounded expression. "Here, I can prove it."

He held out his paw. Nestled in between the five pads of his toes were dozens of tiny granules.

"Ooh. What is it?" Fleabag asked.

"It's kitty litter," Harry replied.

Fleabag sniffed at the grains. "I simply love that exotic smell."

"I believe it's cat wee."

Fleabag took another deep breath. "Rub your paw on the ground. I want to roll in it."

Junior grabbed Harry's paw. "Hold on. Before you dispose of the evidence."

He took a moment to sniff the grains. The scent was weak but definable. It was *definitely* wee. But from an animal he had never met before.

"I'd still like further proof that you found Cat World," Junior said.

"Stop being negative," Fleabag told Junior. Then she turned to Harry. "Tell us what happened, Harry. And I want to hear every single detail."

Chapter 14

CONFESSIONS

GRIZZLY was growing impatient. Ever since
an elderly Great Dane named Shan had told
him the truth about Cat World, he had spent
every waking minute searching for the place.
Shan had also mentioned that cats were crafty
and experts at hiding. Grizzly had replied that
finding the cats would be a cinch.

Yet, Grizzly had been searching for a week
now, and the loathsome creatures had still
managed to avoid his detection.

"Here, kitty kitty," Grizzly whispered. "Come out, come out, wherever you are."

He walked alone today. This mission required stealth, and last night Diesel and Chain had made more noise than a herd of elephants in a peanut factory. In fact, they had made so much noise, Grizzly was sure the cats were now aware the big dogs were looking for them.

And that might cause them to seal the entrances or move. Time was running out.

If the secret entrance to Cat World continued to elude Grizzly, he'd be forced to extend his search to include Little Rover. It would mean defying Dog Law, but Grizzly was desperate. Finding Cat World was beneficial to all of dog-kind, and therefore worth breaking the law for.

Besides, Dog Law stank. It was time for some new rules, he thought.

Of course, the problem was that Grizzly didn't know much about cats. He was relying on his great tracking skills to detect the scent of something so unusual it could *only* belong to a cat.

No dog Grizzly knew had seen a cat before.

Shan had, the oldest dog in Big Rover. Shan happened to be Grizzly's mother. She was also the dog who had told Grizzly about the cats.

It had been a week ago when Shan had called Grizzly into her kennel. He remembered it as easily as if it had been that morning.

"Sit down, my son," Shan had said. "I am an old dog, and my time of passing is drawing near."

"Nonsense," Grizzly replied with a snort. "You have plenty of years left."

Shan coughed. "No matter. It is time you learned the truth I have kept a secret for many years. It is the truth about cats."

Grizzly growled. "Cats are extinct."

"Cats are not extinct. I told you that for their safety. I made a promise a long time ago to never reveal their existence or whereabouts."

"Then tell me where they are hiding."

His mother shook her head. "I cannot. Finding them is something you must do on your own."

He thumped his paw on the ground. "Tell me, Mother. I demand to know everything. I am the leader of the big dogs. As leader, I must know the truth of everything!"

Shan stared into his eyes. Then she shook her head. "You are too angry to listen to the truth. I should not have mentioned the cats. Forget what I said. Cats are extinct. Let's leave it at that."

"You're right, I am angry," Grizzly said. "Either you have been lying to me my whole life or you are lying to me now. Which is it?"

Instead of answering, Shan gave him a smile and she patted the bed for Grizzly to sit beside her.

He did as she asked.

"Forget about the cats," she said. "You should be training for the Dog Paddle Challenge. It's a little over a week away. Just because you've won three years in a row is no reason to get lazy."

"I'm in perfect shape," Grizzly said. "And you're changing the subject. Why are the cats hidden?"

When Shan sighed, it was like listening to a wooden box sealed a long time ago finally being opened. Grizzly knew his mother was old, but it wasn't until now that he understood *how* old.

He rested his head against hers and said in

a gentle voice, "Mother, I am the leader of the big dogs now. A great leader requires great knowledge. If there is anything I need to know, you should tell me."

Shan nodded. "Yes, this secret is part of your legacy. Fur enough, I will tell you all you need to know about cats."

Then Grizzly's mother spent all morning telling him about the dogs and cats of the old times. And how they had once lived together.

She told him of the story of how it came to be that small dogs lived in Little Rover and big dogs in Big Rover.

She told him many things that no dog had ever heard in a long, long time.

But she would not tell him the one thing that plagued him in his sleep.

How to find Cat World.

Chapter 15

CRYING OVER SPILT MILK

BEAUREGARD, the oldest cat in Cat World, lay in his bed with a soft blanket pulled up to his chin. His daughter, Anastasia, carried a bowl of lukewarm milk to him.

"Here's my favourite girl," Beauregard croaked as Anastasia swaggered up to him. "Come to give a dying cat a hug."

Anastasia planted a kiss on the top of his head.

"Oh, do stop talking nonsense, Father,"

she said. "You have a cold, that's all. If you came with me to the surface and let the sun warm your bones you'd feel better in no time."

"The surface is no place for a cat," Beauregard said sternly.

"One day of basking in the sun will clear up your cold faster than a full week in bed with round-the-clock fish-head soup."

Beauregard shook his head. "My dear girl, if you were to get caught on the surface—"

He stopped short. To dwell on the trouble his daughter would get into if she was discovered on the surface brought a tear to his eye. And the extent of the trouble would depend on who found her first: cat or dog.

It hadn't always been that way, he mused. But ever since cats had outlawed collars, baths, and anything else resembling a rule, they seemed to have thrown caution to the wind. Remaining underground during the day, however, was the one rule the cats aimed to abide by, for their own safety.

Dogs believed cats to be extinct. Beauregard believed that the discovery of cats by the dogs would create a media circus. He suspected that every dog would camp outside of every drain, tunnel, and cellar to snatch a look at them.

The cats would never have another moment's privacy.

Beauregard was more than happy to let the dogs remain oblivious to their existence. Forever, preferably. Yet he could sense the young cats growing restless. They wanted *more*, demanding things other than warm milk and non-stop games.

The definition of *more* wasn't clear. But it was clear the young cats wanted change.

And his daughter, Anastasia, was chief amongst the radicals.

He watched as Anastasia busied herself by adjusting the old cat's blanket and pillow. A delay tactic, he guessed. She was here to badger him into going up to the surface.

"It's too dark and too cold down here," she said.

"But it's safe."

"There are no windows to feel the breeze or the sun. No windows to see the stars or the moon."

This was not a new argument.

"We are safe," he said.

"I hate it down here," she added.

"This is where we live."

"No father, this is where *you* live. Why should I have to suffer?"

"You have food and shelter. I'd hardly call that suffering."

Anastasia narrowed her eyes. "Prisoners get food and shelter."

She walked around him, flicking her tail. A sly tone crept into her voice. "There are other cats who feel the same way I do."

"You must stop encouraging them, Anastasia. We live down here. Dogs live up there. And that's that."

Beauregard gave his daughter a stern look. For all the good it did. She smiled at him and his heart melted as fast as ice cream on a hot day.

"You're exactly like your mother," he said gently. His voice brimmed with nostalgia and the memory of licking custard off the pavement with Anastasia's mother. "She was as pretty as a sunset and persistent like the westerly wind. Life would have turned out better for you if she was still alive"

"Life would have turned out *differently*,

Father," Anastasia said. "Not necessarily better."

Beauregard nodded and smiled to himself. "Since when did you become a wise old cat?"

"It happened about the same time that I grew whiskers. But you probably had your head over an air purifier at the time. Too busy conjuring up imaginary diseases to notice that I wasn't a kitten anymore."

It was at that moment that Beauregard realised if he had possessed half his daughter's wisdom when he'd been her age, the cats might have the life she now coveted. But his youthful spirit, his *arrogance*, had cast the cats their unfortunate fate.

He shook his head to loosen the cobwebs of old memories.

"I suppose it is time we returned to the surface," Beauregard said with a sigh. "I do miss the feeling of sleeping on a sunny windowsill. Let me think of the best way to handle this."

"Oh, father." Anastasia raced over and gave him a hug, almost choking him. "I know you'll think of something. And after we're free you should take over from Montgomery as leader of the cats."

"Hah!" Beauregard said, a little too harshly that it brought on a fit of coughing. "What an awful job. I enjoy retirement too much and partying too little."

Anastasia swished her tail. "By the way, I almost forgot to tell you something important. A small dog found one of the tunnels leading into Cat World. I had nothing to do with it, I swear. Anyway, Montgomery's going to dog-nap him tonight and try one of his experiments."

"Oh dear, that is bad news, especially for the poor dog. I suppose Montgomery will turn this incident into a big hoo-hah. Balloons. Sparklers. Streamers."

"He does love to entertain," Anastasia agreed. "Will you come, even for a little while? It will do you good to get out of bed."

"No, I think I'll stay here. I need time to think." Beauregard stroked his whiskers. Then he quickly lapped up his milk and held the empty bowl up to his daughter. He gave her a big grin and said, "I think better on a full stomach."

Anastasia laughed out loud. "Oh, father," she said, taking the bowl from him and shaking her head. "Any more cream and you'll be the size of the cow it came from."

How Beauregard loved to hear his daughter's delightful laughter. It broke his heart to think that his actions in the past had played a pivotal role in the imprisonment she now felt.

Anastasia was a member of the Cat World leadership committee. She knew the story behind Cat World, yet she had never once said a bad word against her father for causing this confinement.

He owed it to his daughter to fix his mess.

Plus, it was becoming a little crowded down here. And too noisy, too chaotic.

Yes, it was time the cats were free.

Chapter 16

A SOUR TASTING TRUTH

HARRY had just finished convincing Fleabag and Junior that he was telling the truth about Cat World.

"I'm glad Grizzly ambushed us," Harry said. "Otherwise, I would never have wandered off and found the tunnel."

Suddenly Harry's eyes widened. "I just realised something. This discovery will make me the most famous dog in history."

"I bet that's what Grizzly was looking for,"

Junior said. "Fleabag and I saw him in Big Rover. He was acting suspicious. I thought he had finally had enough of our trespassing, and he was looking for the hole in the fence to board it up. I bet he was looking for Cat World."

Fleabag gasped. "And Harry found it first. Grizzly will be cranky about that."

"Are you two seriously worried about what Grizzly thinks?" Harry scoffed. "Because I'm not. He's nothing but a bully and I'm glad I found Cat World first."

"When are we going to tell the rest of the dogs?" Fleabag asked, her eyes lighting up.

Harry stopped wagging his tail and sat on his haunches. "I've had some time to think about what we tell the other dogs. It might be wise to hold off sharing this news. At least for a few days."

"Why would we do that?" Junior asked.

"I'm sure the cats don't want us all barging in on them," Harry replied.

"I want to see Cat World," Fleabag gushed. "When can we go? Huh, Harry? When?"

"This is precisely my point," Harry said. "The big dogs will want to see Cat World too, and when they do, they're likely to smash it to pieces."

"Why?" Junior asked.

Harry clamped his jaw shut. He hadn't meant to tell them about the statue. Drats to his big mouth.

"Why would the big dogs want to smash up Cat World?" Junior demanded.

"Because that's what big dogs do," Harry snapped.

"Forget about the big dogs," Fleabag said. "Tell me what Cat World looks like."

Harry was eager to change the topic. Still, he had to force himself to shake off the image of the statue. He conjured up pictures of the magical world instead.

His voice took on a whimsical tone as he spoke. "It's dark and cold because it's deep underground. The walls are concrete. The chamber was vast and windowless, so it's like night-time all the time. But there are mirrors everywhere that give off reflective light, enough to see by. The place has a weird smell too, like vinegar and rotten wood. And there must have been thousands of cats in the main room. They were playing all sorts of games. You name it, they were playing it."

"Bingo," Fleabag said with a cheeky grin. Then she nudged Junior.

"Snap," Junior barked.

"Marco Polo."

"Chess."

"Operation."

"Hopscotch."

"Yahtzee."

Harry lifted a paw. "Guys. What are you doing?"

Fleabag chuckled. "You said, 'you name it, they were playing it'. So we're naming the games."

Harry rolled his eyes. "Every dog is a comedian. Anyway, as I was saying, Cat World is noisy with no windows to escape, so every sound echoed. My ears still hurt from the crying, bellowing, and shouting. But the singing, well, that was the worst. It sounded like a blunt power tool grinding through metal."

Harry watched as Junior and Fleabag cringed at his description. (Dogs have sensitive hearing, and they dislike high-pitched sounds. They especially detest those silly whistles that only *they* can hear, and the only reason they come when this whistle is blown is to tell the

Furless Ones to stop it!)

Harry continued: "The cats played their games with wanton abandonment."

"What does wanton abandonment mean?" Fleabag asked, her head tilted to the side.

"It means a reckless neglect of reason," Junior said, knowingly. "It's a hormone imbalance. Obedience training helps dogs grow out of it."

"Pity," Fleabag gushed. "It sounds like fun."

"Will you two quit mucking around and focus on the real issue," Harry said. "You're as bad as Kevin when he spies a ball.

"Sorry, Harry," the two dogs said in unison.

Harry leaned in closer. "The cats were doing all kinds of stuff with reckless abandonment. They were singing, dancing, playing cards, boxing, you name it—" Harry held his paw up to stop Junior and Fleabag taking him so literally. "It was amazing. I had to stop myself from joining in on the fun."

A moment's silence passed by. Then Fleabag started jumping up and down.

"What do the *cats* look like, Harry?" she

asked. "Tell me everything. Are they pretty?"

"In a weird way, you could say they are pretty," Harry said. "Some of them have stripes like a tiger. Others have splotches of colour all over them. Some have dots, some are all one colour. Yet every coat looks as soft as a slipper's lining."

"They sound luxurious," Fleabag said.

"Their faces are flat like a pug dog," Harry continued. "It must be why the place stank to high heaven. With such short snouts it would be impossible for them to notice the stench. And their tails swish from left to right, as quickly as blowflies avoiding bug spray."

Fleabag rolled over and sighed dreamily. "Oh, Harry. They sound exotic."

"They are," he replied. "They have eyes like a lizard's, they're quick like flies, and they're agile too. They did cartwheels and somersaults, and they landed on their feet *every time*."

Fleabag started to drool. "When can we go see them, Harry? When? This evening?"

Harry stiffened. The image of the statue made from puppy teeth flashed in his mind again, and this time it seemed to come to life in his mind. The statue's head moved. It grinned at Harry...

"Tonight's out of the question for me," he said. "I reckon I'll be grounded for a while for being out all night."

"But I want to see the cats," Fleabag squealed. "They sound wonderful."

Harry started to shiver with worry. He couldn't lie to his friends. He couldn't lie to *anybody*. Dogs were incapable of lying.

"They're not as wonderful as you think," he said. He shook his head. "I saw a terrible, terrible sight on my way out of the vast chamber. I can't even talk about it."

Junior put a paw on Harry's shoulder. "What did you see? You can tell us."

What *did* Harry see? He had asked himself that same question a hundred times. A mirage. A phantom. A painting.

The image in his mind returned. This time the giant cat pointed at Harry. Its eyes burned red, and then he heard a mirthless laugh.

He shuddered. "As I was leaving Cat World, I saw a statue. It was of a giant cat. It was milky white and pretty eerie actually." He paused and fidgeted, nervous about continuing.

"Guys, I'd rather we talked about something else."

Junior crossed his paws. Harry knew that look. Junior was getting ready to say, 'I told you so'.

Harry took a deep breath. "All right. But I'm only telling you this because you're my best friends and we don't keep secrets from each other. The statue was made from puppy teeth."

"Puppy teeth!" Junior's growl rumbled inside Harry's kennel. "I told you something bad would happen. Fleabag, did I say last night that something bad would happen?"

Fleabag's face crumpled. Her bottom lip quivered. She looked ready to cry.

"Why would they do that?" she whispered. "Why would they steal our teeth from the Tooth Fairy?"

"We should tell Grizzly," Junior said. "About Cat World. About the statue."

"We can't tell Grizzly *anything*," Harry cried. "He will send an army of dogs into Cat World."

"What's the problem with that? He'll retrieve our teeth."

"I'm sure Grizzly will do a bang-up job of

retrieving our teeth." Harry scowled as a thought occurred to him. "There must be a reason why the cats have the teeth. Isn't that the bigger issue?"

Junior's eyed widened. "You want to find out the reason. I can see it in your eyes. But Harry, this isn't a puzzle to be solved. This is serious."

"I agree. It is serious. Which is why we need to investigate this *before* we tell the big dogs."

Fleabag was almost howling with nervousness. "Do you think they hurt the Tooth Fairy when they stole the puppy teeth?"

Junior banged his paw on the floor. "The biggest issue is that they have turned the teeth into a statue of a cat. Our loyalty is to *all* dogs, big and small. Grizzly needs to know about this. As well as *all* our family and friends."

"Maybe I can tell everyone about Cat World without mentioning the statue," Harry said, lifting his paws in pleading manner.

"It won't matter," Fleabag said, solemnly. "All the dogs will want to see Cat World for themselves. And when they do, they'll see the statue. It's better that we tell them first."

Harry lay down on the floor and he wanted to put his paws over his head. If only he hadn't gone into Big Rover. If only he hadn't stumbled upon the tunnel. If only he hadn't found Cat World. If only he had listened to his friends in the first place and stayed at home.

"You know telling Grizzly's the only way to get our teeth back," Junior urged.

"I know," Harry said with a sigh. "But with the right publicity, I could be famous. Think of the tours I could organize."

Junior scoffed. "You'll be famous, and we'll build a statue of you. Only we'll build it out of cat teeth."

Fleabag leapt up. "Hey, I have an idea. We should ask Old Roger if he can help us decide what to do. He's the wisest dog in Little Rover."

"Clever thinking," Harry said with a nod. "Old Roger is the oldest small dog still alive. He might even remember the time before the cats were extinct."

And more importantly, Harry thought, it would delay him having to tell Grizzly. In a way, Harry was giving the cats one last chance to dismantle the statue. But the cats would never do that willingly. And even Harry knew this.

Chapter 17

UN-FRIENDLY ADVICE

OLD ROGER lived as far south in Little Rover as you could get, at the southern end of Fat Belly Road on a street that was lined with pine trees. His house was close to the canal that ran out to sea. Some days, when the tide was a long time between going out and coming in, the smell of decaying seaweed was the strongest.

Had he known the three small dogs were marching toward his home, he might have taken that moment to hide under the house.

When Old Roger heard the barks calling to him, he ignored them. The yapping continued.

It took a while for Old Roger to come to the door. His eyesight was diminished, and he had to push his face into the flyscreen mesh. The tiny squares of nylon obscured his vision. He couldn't be sure if there were one or ten dogs standing at his front gate. By all the yapping, it sounded like ten.

"Who goes there?" he barked.

"It's Harry, Junior, and Fleabag. Sorry to bother you—"

"What do you want?" Old Roger pushed through the doggy door. His hearing was as dismal as his vision, but it was his tired old bones that stopped him going to the gate. "And speak up."

"Sorry to bother you," Harry shouted, "but we have something very important to tell you."

"You can tell me from there," Old Roger snapped at them. He was ready to go back to bed.

"It's too risky to talk out here," Harry said. "May we come up?"

Old Roger stared out at the blurry shapes. He knew who these dogs were. Old Roger knew every dog in Little Rover. He'd heard stories about these three. They were well-liked and trusted by all the dogs in Little Rover. But Old Roger sensed they were bringing trouble.

"Come up to the porch," Old Roger said. "And it had better be important."

The three dogs trotted up the path and stepped up onto the porch.

Old Roger waited for them to speak. They were silent.

"Speak up then." Old Roger thumped the ground with his paw. "Street signs tell you information without talking. You're not street signs. And I couldn't read you if you were. You have three seconds to tell me what's so urgent that you feel the need to disturb my nap."

"There's no easy way to say this," Harry said. "So I guess I'll come straight out and say it. I found Cat World."

Old Roger waved the dogs up to the front porch. They trotted up and he glared at them.

"You dare to defy Dog Law in front of me?" he cried.

"No, sir," Harry said.

"Cat World doesn't exist. Cats are extinct. Go home and repeat Dog Law twenty times.

That ought to curb you of your lying."

"I'm not lying," Harry said, striking a paw against the ground in defiance. "I found Cat World. I saw the cats—"

Old Roger lifted his paw to silence the dog.

He turned to speak to the other two small dogs. "Did you see this place?"

"Yikes, no," Fleabag cried.

Junior lowered his head. "No, sir."

"I promise you I'm not lying," Harry said. "There was a tunnel, and then I stepped into a room full of cats—"

Old Roger lunged at Harry. "Where was this tunnel?"

Harry froze. "Ah, it was in the forest."

"In the forest that you are strictly forbidden to enter?"

Harry nodded slowly.

Old Roger leaned in close. "In the forest that is on the other side of Big Rover that you are *also* forbidden to enter?"

"Yes, sir," said Harry in a sheepish voice.

"That is three rules you have broken," Old Roger said. "I have no time for law breakers. Leave, and never return."

Old Roger turned and headed for the

house. He stopped at the doggy door, and over his shoulder he gave the dogs a stern look.

"You will never speak to anyone about what you told me. Cats are extinct."

Then Old Roger stepped through the doggy door and returned to his basket, cranky that the dogs had brought up the subject of cats. He could hardy remember what a cat looked like anymore. His memory had become faded, frosted over by Father Time so wholly that it resembled a grimy window.

With enough rubbing at his eyes, he was able to wear through a tiny piece of dirt encrusted into his memory bank. If he squinted, he could make out the image of a cat.

Swishy-tailed beasts, with pointy teeth, who were loyal only to them themselves. They were also crafty and clever and capable of tricking dogs into doing something that would get them into trouble.

This discovery of Cat World was no accident, Old Roger thought.

No accident at all.

The cats were up to something.

To say Old Roger had been shocked when Harry had announced he'd located Cat World was an understatement. Old Roger had almost fainted. He'd never thought he'd live to see the day when cats would become *un*-extinct.

Worse still, the discovery of Cat World opened a far bigger can of worms than the unearthing of a creature thought to be wiped out.

Because, what lived beneath the surface was more than a horde of ruffian, misfit cats.

There were secrets in Cat World.

Secrets that Old Roger had hoped would remain hidden for ever.

Chapter 18

DÉJÀ POO (OR I'VE HAD THIS FEELING BEFORE)

HARRY and the other two small dogs left Old Roger's front porch. They headed north along the dirt track that led to the jetty, stomping in frustration through the front gardens of the waterfront houses. The scent of pine lessened the nearer they got to Buster Bay, and they were glad to leave the heavy perfume behind. From now on Harry would associate the smell of pine with failure.

When they arrived at Buster Bay, they stopped. Then they gazed into the deep green water, seeing nothing, yet unable to avert their gaze. Harry was hoping an answer to his problem would pop out above a wave. All he saw were dolphins and schools of silver fish and the odd fishing boat.

Each dog was deep in their thoughts.

Fleabag broke the silence when she said, "Well, that was as pleasant as sliding on sandpaper."

Harry tore his gaze away from the hypnotic sheet of water. "You do believe me, don't you? I really did find Cat World."

"I believe you, Harry," Junior said with a nod. "Old Roger was too quick to dismiss the idea. That makes me think he knows more than he's telling."

"It is all very suspicious," Fleabag said. "If Grizzly was looking for the cats, he also knows more than he's letting on."

"Whatever we decide to do we'll need to do it quickly," Harry said. "Cat World will be in real trouble if Grizzly finds them before we can unravel this mystery."

Junior's face was pinched in distress.

"Why would you want to protect the cats? What they have done with our teeth is unforgivable."

Harry sighed. "There's something familiar about Cat World. It has puzzled me all morning. It's been tickling me at the back of my head."

"It's probably a flea," Fleabag said.

"I mean on the inside," Harry replied.

"Oh. Worms, then."

"Fleabag, will you let me explain? I have this weird feeling that I've been to Cat World before."

"That's impossible, Harry. You've only just discovered it."

"I know. But I had a dream the other night, only now I'm thinking it wasn't a dream but a repressed memory. If Cat World is destroyed, so is the evidence."

"Fur enough, we'll do this your way," Junior said, begrudgingly. "But as soon as we've uncovered this riddle, we *will* tell Grizzly."

A twig snapped behind them. The small dogs jumped and barked involuntarily.

When they turned around, Grizzly was standing behind them. His sneer was as menacing as a wolf at the door of a house made from straw. And even though it was late in the afternoon, his immense size cast the biggest shadow. It made the sky disappear.

"You have something to tell me," Grizzly said. "Go ahead and tell me. And don't leave out any of the juicy bits."

Chapter 19

AN ULTIMATUM

GRIZZLY couldn't stop the grin spreading across his face. The small dogs were starting to shake.

"Spill it, dirt bags. What are you going to tell me?"

Fleabag was the first to react.

"We've got something to tell you all right," she barked. "You're trespassing on small dog property."

The place where they stood, on the shore

of Buster Bay, was far from the border separating the two towns. And even though Grizzly was in direct violation of Dog Law, he wasn't concerned with this. For a good reason.

"You lot are forbidden from entering Big Rover," Grizzly replied. He lifted his lips in a sneer. "Yes, I know about your nightly visits into my town. I'd say we're even. Besides, I'm willing to overlook your numerous violations if you tell me what you three mini-mutts are conspiring about."

Harry titled his head. "You call this conspiring? We're taking in the view, that's all."

"It ain't nice to lie to big dogs," Grizzly said. "Just tell me your little secret and I'll be on my way."

"Secret?" Harry shook his head. "We don't have a secret. You've spent too long in the sun, Grizzly. You're delirious with dehydration."

Grizzly stared at Harry. The small dogs ought to have known better than to argue with a big dog. Grizzly was well-trained in the art of all types of combat. He would win at any game of rough and tumble. Even in a game of three against one, Grizzly would win.

Grizzly took a step closer. "Tell me

everything you know about Cat World. Tell me where to find it."

Harry gulped. Then he let out a nervous chuckle. "What a preposterous thing to say. I've never heard of Cat World."

"Yeah, ya big dummy," Fleabag added. "Every dog knows cats are extinct?"

"Every dog except you three," Grizzly said with a sly grin. "I overheard you talking to Old Roger. You know where Cat World is. And you're going to tell me how to find it."

"Why should I tell you anything?" Harry asked.

Grizzly's sinister smile grew even more sinister. "Because if you don't, there will be trouble."

***

HARRY gasped. He had expected that Grizzly would resort to violence. And if Grizzly was this angry now, how angry would he be when he knew about the puppy teeth?

The cats wouldn't stand a chance against the big dogs. And Harry couldn't be responsible for this destruction.

"I'll never tell you," Harry said defiantly. "So you'll never be able to harm them."

Grizzly licked his teeth. "If Cat World remains undamaged, then Little Rover will be smashed to pieces instead. Take your pick."

"I think he means it," Junior whispered to Harry. "You'd better tell him."

Harry shook his head. "No. There must be another way to resolve this."

"Please," Fleabag begged. "He'll destroy Little Rover. We can't fight the big dogs. No matter how brave we are, it's a fight we can never win."

Harry faced Grizzly as if he was bracing himself against a fierce wind. "Surely we can negotiate. Is there something else you'd rather have instead? I know where there's a secret stash of bones the size of your leg."

Grizzly lunged at the small dogs, snapping his jaw. "Tell me where Cat World is so I can retrieve our puppy teeth?"

This statement caught Harry completely unawares. He felt his insides quiver with fright. "I never said anything to Old Roger about puppy teeth."

Grizzly snorted hot air through his nose. "I

know more than you think. Those cats have something that belongs to us, Harry. And I want it back."

Grizzly leaned in close enough for Harry to know he'd had a beef and pickle sandwich for lunch. Harry refused to flinch. While it was completely reasonable to feel fear, it was inviting death to show it.

"I'll let you be in the lead team when we go in and destroy the place," Grizzly said. "How about it, champ?"

"Tell him, Harry," Junior said.

"Yes, tell him, Harry." Fleabag nudged him. "I'll never sleep again knowing the cats have our puppy teeth."

"How much do you know about the puppy teeth?" Harry asked Grizzly.

"They stole them. I want them back."

"But do you know *why* they have them?"

"Does it matter?"

Harry pictured the glistening statue in his mind. If he was the first dog to have visited Cat World, it stood to reason that Grizzly didn't know what the cats had done with the puppy teeth. Although how Grizzly even knew about Cat World was a mystery.

Another mystery for another day, Harry thought. He'd made up his mind that he would ask the cats to dismantle the statue and return the teeth, and only *then* would he tell the rest of the dogs about Cat World.

"Are you a betting dog, Harry?" Grizzly asked, snapping Harry out of his thoughts. "Because you seem to be willing to bet that I'm toying with you right now. Let me assure you, I am deadly serious."

"Can you at least give me until high noon tomorrow?" Harry asked.

That would buy him time to speak with the cats. At least they could explain how they'd ended up with the puppy teeth.

Grizzly nodded. "Fur enough. I like a dog with gumption. But you had better tell me what I want to know tomorrow at noon, and no tricks. My temper is hard to control when I'm angry."

Without delay the big dog turned around, trotting back to his side of town. Only now did Harry catch a glimpse of the rest of the big dogs who had been skulking behind the boat sheds. Some were sniffing along the bottom of the fence that was the borderline of Dog Town.

Some were digging in the sand beneath the jetty.

One thing was certain. They were searching for Cat World. It was only a matter of time before they found it.

Grizzly was well out of sight by now. Harry let out the breath he'd been holding.

"Wow, we've never had an old-fashioned stand-off in Little Rover before," Harry said, jokingly.

But when he received no scathing remark from Junior, he turned and saw his two friends were already at the end of the Chew Toy Lane and getting ready to cross onto Mongrel Street. They were heading home without him.

"Fleabag? Junior? Wait up." Harry trotted ahead and caught up with the two dogs "Hey, what's up?"

Junior and Fleabag kept on walking. Harry sensed they were ignoring him. After all, dogs have excellent hearing and he was standing right next to them. But his friends kept their gazes averted and their noses held high in the air.

"Guys, what's going on?"

"Go away, Harry," Junior said, coldly. "In

case you're too dumb to figure it out, Fleabag and I are ignoring you."

"Aw, are you mad at me over what Grizzly said? He's highly unlikely to destroy Little Rover. Even Grizzly has to realise something like that involves too much paperwork."

Junior finally turned to look at Harry. His face was screwed up, the way the bottom end of a capsicum is all bent in on itself.

"You've finally gone and done it, Harry," Junior said crankily. "You've put Little Rover at risk over a selfish desire to compete against the big dogs. And over a bunch of cats that ought to be punished anyway."

"But... but," Harry faltered, "no matter what the cats have done, nobody deserves to have their homes destroyed."

Fleabag whirled around. "We don't deserve to have our homes destroyed either."

Chapter 20

THE BEARER OF BAD NEWS

ANASTASIA watched the big dogs and little dogs on the beach. Her father had said it was dangerous on the surface, and she agreed. That was why she was spying on the dogs from the top of a flat-roofed shed that for most of the year was home to azure-blue rowboats and mud-brown rats.

The roof height made the shed the perfect vantage point to keep tabs on her enemy. Her whiskers usually tingled whenever the dogs came too close anyway. Right now, her whiskers were making her cheeks hotter than sunburn, and it wasn't because she was sitting right on top of the dogs.

Anastasia had overheard Grizzly's threat to destroy Cat World. And when Harry had refused to expose the location, Grizzly had threatened to destroy Little Rover.

Anastasia wanted her freedom, but not at the expense of her home or the home of the small dogs. She also didn't want the alternative, which was to be stuck underground for the rest of her life.

A bang in the distance scared the living daylights out of her. She had to get home and warn the cats.

She waited until most of the dogs had disappeared before sliding down the side of the boat shed. Then she raced like the wind across a grassed area until she came upon a storm water drain that led her home.

She found Montgomery, the leader of Cat World, in his basket.

She explained what she had overheard at the beach.

"What do we do?" Anastasia asked him.

"Do we give the dogs back their teeth?"

"That would be a mistake," Montgomery said. "They are legally ours to take. It is their problem that they don't know their own history. Not ours."

"But the big dogs mean to destroy us."

"Only if the small dog tells him the location. I will plan a defence against such an occurrence."

"How?"

Montgomery hopped down from his bed and flicked his tail. Then he strode over to stand in front of a mirror, admiring his reflection. (Where Harry had thought the mirrors were there to reflect light, they were actually placed around the walls, giving the cats an uninterrupted, three-hundred-and-sixty-degree glimpse of themselves.)

Anastasia pounced in front of Montgomery. "Hey, pay attention. How will you stop this?"

"I will dog-nap this trouble-maker and give him my memory erasing elixir."

Anastasia rolled her eyes. Montgomery was always concocting some potion or another.

"Perhaps it would be easier to dismantle

the statue," she said.

Montgomery whirled on her. "Absolutely not. We can do what we wish with the teeth once we claim them. The statue remains. In fact, I already have plans for a second statue."

Inwardly, Anastasia groaned. She hated that statue. Maybe letting the dogs destroy it was for the best.

Except they would destroy everything else too.

Chapter 21

IN THE SLAMMER

MONTGOMERY had the fluffiest of tails, and it now twitched with excitement that his mission to dog-nap Harry was a great success.

"Wake up the dog," Montgomery ordered.

Two cats shook Harry until he began barking loudly.

Anastasia, who had demanded she be part of the crew to dog-nap Harry, removed the cloth tied across the small dog's face.

"Was a blindfold really necessary,

Montgomery?" she asked. "He already knows how to find us."

"We can never be too careful where dogs are concerned." And just to be extra careful, Montgomery took one step back.

"I am Montgomery, leader of Cat World," he sang out. "King of the kitties. Pharaoh of the felines. Lord of the lions. Prince of the pussies. Master of the mousers—"

Anastasia coughed from behind.

"Who are you?" Montgomery demanded of the dog.

"I am Harry."

"Yes, but what do you reign supreme over?"

"Nothing. Just my kennel."

Montgomery chuckled. "Just your kennel. You have no subordinates? No underlings?" Montgomery felt his grin widen. "No *dogsbodies?*"

"No. I have friends."

Montgomery swatted a paw in the air. "Do you know why you're here, Harry?"

"No, but I get the feeling you're going to tell me?"

The dog pulled on the restraints tied

around his four paws.

"It won't work," Montgomery said. "Those restraints are cat collars that have never been worn, therefore they are as strong as the day they came off the production line."

Harry growled. "Why are you holding me prisoner?"

"Because that is what we do with our enemies," Montgomery said. "You broke into our home and now Grizzly wants to destroy it. That makes *you* my enemy."

"Grizzly is bluffing," Harry said. "He'll never go through with it."

"My source tells me he has threatened to destroy Little Rover if you refuse to tell him our whereabouts. I hardly think you'll choose your home over ours. My source also tells me that you have until noon tomorrow to tell him. I have decided to keep you here until *after* noon. Therefore, you will be unable to tell him."

"My absence won't stop Grizzly searching for Cat World."

"No. But it will give us enough time to seal all the exits and entrances. No dog can get in."

"And no cat can get out," Anastasia said with a gasp.

Montgomery jabbed a claw at her. "That is your doing, Anastasia. I know all about your visits to the surface. You have played a part in attracting the attention of the dogs. You will immediately cease your visits to the surface. Grizzly must never be able to pick up your scent."

"I wasn't going to tell Grizzly how to get into Cat World," Harry said.

Montgomery whirled on him. "And to make sure of it, I have prepared a batch of my special elixir. It will erase your memory. But first we shall sing a song."

Montgomery clapped his hands twice in quick succession. Taking their cue, the cats that were concealed in the shadows, picked up their upturned saucepans-for-instruments, stepped out into the light, and began beating out a tune.

Then they began to sing:

Dogs cannot climb up trees
Nor can they wash themselves
So what the heck are dogs good for?
Nothing!
Yes, they can do stupid tricks

If fetch is what you fancy,
We'd rather sit beside the fire'n do
Nothing!
Heel and fetch and roll over
How totally degrading
So what is it cats learn from dogs?
Nothing!
As cats we are superior
Our intellect astounding
What has a dog between his ears?
Nothing!
I say again, nothing!
Let me hear you sing it
Nothing, nothing, nothing!

The song ended on a note, high enough to have broken glass windows if there had been any. And when the cats applauded, it was deafening, rebounding and rolling around the concrete chamber as loudly as thunder might if it was bottled and released inside a steel drum. Montgomery bowed, and handfuls of kitty litter were tossed into the air.

Harry, however, wore a scowl. "That is a total misrepresentation. Dogs are nothing like that."

Montgomery shrugged his shoulders. "Yes, you *would* say that."

He unscrewed a jar that was sitting on the small table and dipped a teaspoon inside. "This magic broth will make you forget the whereabouts of our secret entrance."

Harry licked his lips. Montgomery knew that the dog was helpless against the impulse to eat anything on offer. It was in a dog's genes to drool over food, whether he liked what was on offer or not.

Montgomery wasn't giving Harry any chance to decide if he liked what was on offer. He waved a paw and two cats sprang out of the darkness to pounce on Harry. They held his jaw wide open while Montgomery poured a thick, yellow liquid down his throat.

Then a hundred sets of amber-coloured eyes watched for a reaction.

Harry's face twisted as the tart flavour made its way down his throat.

Montgomery raised the teaspoon and waved it at Harry. "Another mouthful?"

"No thanks," Harry said with a cough. "I'd rather eat duck poo."

Montgomery tilted his head. "Perhaps that's what my recipe is lacking. Never mind. Soon you will forget everything. You'll forget about the potion, the dog-napping, even the moment leading up to the moment you found the tunnel."

The room full of cats watched in eager expectation, some moving their lips as though chanting a magic spell.

A minute passed by. Then another.

After ten minutes, Harry asked, "How long will this take to work?"

"The effects are immediate," Montgomery said, confusion causing his white fluffy tail to flick madly.

"No offence," Harry said, "but I think your potion is defective. I still remember how to find Cat World. It's halfway up the embankment leading to the wild forest. It's concealed by a fern, and to get there I go behind the blue dumpster in the wrecking yard inside Big Rover."

The cats gasped and spat and hissed.

Montgomery's tail twitched feverishly.

"Hush," he cried out with his arms held high into the air. "You must never say it out loud, even in jest."

"What I'd like to forget," Harry said with a grin, "is your singing. My ears ache from all that screeching."

And because Montgomery was irate that his magical potion had failed to work, and because he was angry that Harry had insulted his vocal talents, he hit Harry on the head with a stale stick of bread.

He knocked the small dog out cold.

Chapter 22

AN UNLIKELY ALLIANCE

HARRY woke up. He was alone in Cat World and sitting facing the statue. Was it his imagination, he wondered, or did the statue bear a striking resemblance to Montgomery?

At least he was free of the restraints that had been digging into his paws. Rubbing at the welts, Harry sensed there was someone else in the room.

He realised he was right, when a shadow peeled itself off the wall and approached him. It moved toward him, bringing with it yellow eyes shaped like a football. The shadow with yellow eyes stopped an inch away from Harry's snout.

"Hello, Harry," the shadow said.

Harry saw that it was a cat. And because he was a well-mannered dog, he said: "Hello."

"I'm Anastasia."

The cat stared long and hard at Harry, as if Harry was supposed to have done something, which from the look on the cat's face he had clearly forgotten to do.

Finally, she said, in a shrill voice (because that's how all cats speak), "I'm your guide home."

"But I already know how to get home."

Anastasia flicked her tail at his nose. She turned toward the archway.

"Coming?" she asked.

By now she was already halfway to the tunnel. Not wanting to spend another second in this underground chamber of horrors, Harry sped off after her. They walked along the tunnel in silence, even though Harry had millions of questions he wanted to ask. But he was stumped with where to begin. He wanted to ask how the cats had ended up underground. He wanted to know why the cats, and not the Tooth Fairy, had their puppy teeth. And most importantly, he wanted to ask why the other cats let Montgomery lead them in a singalong when the fluffy cat clearly couldn't sing.

But for the first time, perhaps ever in his life, Harry was truly mystified. He was ordinarily a dog of action. He usually had a destination, even if he lacked a plan on how to get there. He did things because they were there to be done, preferring to leave the rhyme and reason to Junior and Fleabag. But his best friends had stopped talking to him after he'd refused to tell Grizzly the location of Cat World. Perhaps that was why he was feeling so indecisive, he thought.

"You're terrible at playing spy games," Anastasia said, interrupting Harry's thoughts. "You could have told Montgomery that his potion had worked, and he'd be none the wiser."

"But that would have been a lie. Dogs believe it is wrong to tell lies," Harry said.

"Is that so? Then how come you lied to Grizzly about the statue?"

"That was an omission. An omission of the truth is different to a lie."

Deep in thought, Harry tried to match the smells to scents from home. For example, the sweet smell of damp earth was like a wet towel. The scent of strange animal droppings was like the time a flock of seagulls had invaded his yard after a bag of hot chips had been spilled. And the pungent aroma of ammonia, which he now knew to be cat pee, smelt like the pool water from the house behind his.

Today was turning into a crazy mixed up day full of new things. He wasn't sure he liked straying from routine.

"What sort of cat are you?" he asked.

"I'm just a regular black cat," Anastasia answered.

She gave Harry an odd look. He guessed she was trying to figure out what sort of dog he was, so he said, "I'm a regular brown dog. I don't know what breed I am."

"I know what sort of dog you are."

"You do?"

"You're a good dog."

That made him smile. "Have you always lived underground?"

"For as long as I can remember."

Harry went quiet for a second. Then he

said, "Big dogs live in Big Rover and small dogs live in Little Rover. It's Dog Law."

"I'm well aware of Dog Law," Anastasia explained. "I know more about your kind than you think."

"And yet we know nothing about your kind. Why do you live apart from us? I know that dogs live apart because we dislike each other. Big dogs are too rowdy. Small dogs are too snappy. It's in our DNA. Maybe cats live down here because cats and dogs also dislike each other."

"That's possible. Montgomery seems to think so. He's always telling us how we're supposed to dislike dogs."

Harry nodded. "Then I guess I'm supposed to hate cats. And I guess I should be thankful that Grizzly wants to destroy Cat World. My friends seem to think I should let him."

"That is a natural conclusion. A statue made from your teeth is enough to make any dog bark-raving mad."

Harry shuddered. "That is true. I had plenty of opportunity to alert the big dogs to your presence the night I found the tunnel. But I didn't."

Anastasia swished her tail. "It was very un-doglike of you to have declined your dog-given right."

"Perhaps what's strangest of all is that I like cats," Harry said, speaking as if he was trying to convince himself of this.

Anastasia smiled. "What's strange about that? I like dogs."

Harry had run out of questions for the moment. He continued walking along the tunnel in silence. When the air grew cool, he knew they had come to the end.

"Wait here," Anastasia said. "I'll make sure the coast is clear."

She poked her head outside then waved a paw at Harry.

He followed her out onto the grassy embankment. It was dark outside. The night sky was filled with stars. It was warm, yet a gentle breeze tickled his fur.

Harry turned his head to gaze at the embankment, where the tunnel was hidden from view by the thicket of ferns. The faint breeze hardly moved the foliage at all. Had the wind not suddenly whooshed up last night, Harry would never have found the secret entrance.

"Okay, I'll admit an omission is the same as telling a lie," Harry said in reply to her earlier statement. "But I had to lie to Grizzly. If he knew about the statue, he'd have torn Dog Town apart long ago looking for that entrance."

"He'll find it one day," Anastasia said. She sat on her backside and began licking her paws.

"That's what worries me," Harry said, a quiver in his voice. "Should we board up the tunnel?"

"It won't stop him from finding us." Anastasia stopped licking her paws and gazed up at the sky. "The sky is the most beautiful sight. And the stars." She sighed. "I could look at them forever. But it's the sun I miss the most."

Harry followed her gaze. "I guess the stars are okay."

"Oh, Harry. You've got to see it from where I'm looking. To me, and many other cats, the sky represents freedom. We live in a prison down there."

She stared at the stars with such longing, Harry was reminded of the time someone had moved his favourite chew-toy out of reach.

He had no idea how to console a cat, but her sadness was making him feel sad.

"At least you have fewer rules to follow," Harry offered, hoping to cheer her up. "I'm always getting into trouble. Right now, I'm breaking two Dog Law rules by wandering around at night *and* being in big dog territory. Cats can do whatever they like."

"Except live on the surface," Anastasia whispered.

Harry was too tired to disagree. Montgomery's magic broth had finally kicked in and he was becoming drowsy. He settled down on the grass and closed his eyes. If he was lucky, the elixir would work while he slept, and tomorrow he would wake up and remember nothing.

Suddenly Harry felt a great weight pressing down on his back. He felt his ears were being pulled and twisted.

"Wake up, sleepy head," Anastasia sang out. She laughed out loud and bit his ears. Then she blew a raspberry on his nose and stuck her toes up his nostrils.

"Hey, what was that for?" Harry cried.

Instead of answering Anastasia tickled

him under the armpits.

"Stop it," Harry said, giggling. "I'm ticklish."

Anastasia tickled him harder, but he found it impossible to do anything other than wriggle like a snake. The cat kept laughing while she tormented him, tickling and poking and pulling his tail. Harry could barely stop himself from giggling, much less yell at her to stop. Finally, he managed to wiggle his way out from under her.

He jumped up. But the cat was just as quick. She pounced on him, this time licking his face while she pinned him down. And cats have rough tongues, so the more she licked, the more it tickled.

"Please," Harry said in between fits of laughter. "Stop tickling me."

This time he squirmed hard enough to send Anastasia flying. Yet because she was a cat, she twisted her body mid-flight and landed precisely where she wanted to.

"How do you do that?" Harry asked in awe.

She didn't answer. Instead she ran along the top of the embankment, yelling, "You will never catch me."

"Oh, yes I will."

Harry tore off after her. He was the fastest dog in Little Rover and no way was he going to be beaten in a race by a cat.

Harry quickly caught up to Anastasia. He lunged and landed on top of her with a walloping thud. They rolled down the hill together, wrapped up like a tight ball of wool.

When they crashed into a fallen log, they came apart. Still laughing, Anastasia grabbed a handful of dandelion flowers and threw them at Harry.

He responded by grabbing her tail with his teeth, gentle enough that her skin was left unbroken, but hard enough that she couldn't run away.

Then he sat down on his haunches, grinning at her as she wrestled to escape. When she swiped at him with her claws, he immediately let go.

He leapt up. "That's not fair. You fight dirty."

Anastasia swished her tail and hissed.

Harry growled and forced his hackles to rise.

They stood facing one another, hissing and growling like sworn enemies, until suddenly they burst into a fit of hysterical laughter.

"That was fun," Anastasia said. "Want to play some more?"

Harry almost said yes. But it was late. "You should get back before Montgomery thinks I've cat-napped you. I've caused enough trouble already."

Anastasia sat down to groom her coat, removing grass clippings and dead bugs from her fur. Then she stared thoughtfully at Harry.

"You really don't remember me, do you?" she asked.

"Why should I remember you?"

"We met a long time ago."

"I think I'd remember that."

"Maybe it will come to you in your dreams," Anastasia said.

She leapt up into the air. Her black coat merged into the night sky.

She was gone.

Harry headed home.

Chapter 23

PATROL DOGS

GRIZZLY preferred searching in the dark. His senses worked best in the hours when there was minimal disturbance from the sounds and smells brought on by the Furless Ones. But now he realised that daytime was better for searching, because he and his friends, Diesel and Chain, could make as much noise as they liked while they searched for Cat World.

It was the next day, and Grizzly and his henchdogs were patrolling Big Rover.

Diesel pulled his head out from behind a pile of tyres. "Why are we still looking for these cats? Harry will tell you where they are at noon. That was the deadline you gave him."

"I'll tell you why we're looking for Cat World," Grizzly said with a snarl. "*I* want to be the one to find it, and I want to be the one to destroy the cats and their home for stealing our puppy teeth. Is it wrong to expect a little support in what will be the single biggest claim to fame in all of dog-kind?"

He paused to allow his words to sink in. The meaning sunk into Diesel's head faster than it did Chain's, yet it got there in the end. And the two dogs smiled with menacing glee.

"We're gonna be famous," they sang simultaneously.

"That's right, boys. Fame and fortune come to those who work hard to get it. Now, go get it!"

Chapter 24

INVASION

HARRY woke up when he heard a tapping on his kennel door. It was Kevin.

"You'd better come quickly, Harry," Kevin said. "Grizzly is at Buster Bay and he's asking for you."

Not only was Grizzly at Buster Bay, but the entire population of Dog Town was there as well. Hundreds of dogs were gathered on the shore. They were huddled in packs, sniffing at bottoms, arguing over nothing, and urinating on top of one another so that patches of grass died within a matter of seconds.

"What's everyone doing here?" Harry asked, pushing his way through the crowd.

"It's an old-fashioned stand-off," a voice from within the crowd said.

"As long as it doesn't turn into a rumble," another said. "If those big dogs start getting too rowdy, I'm going home."

Fleabag came running toward Harry. "Turn around, Harry. Go home quickly. We'll pretend we never saw you."

Junior was at her side, his eyes wide in panic. "We'll tell Grizzly you were taken to the vet early this morning. We'll tell him you've got Dog Flu. He'll never come near you again."

"Yes, yes," Fleabag said, nodding. "If you're missing, nobody can blame you for refusing to tell him what he wants to know."

"We'll disperse the crowd somehow," Junior added.

"Great biscuit," Harry said with a smile, "for two dogs bent on ignoring me, you sure are doing an awful lot of yappity-yap-yapping."

"Well," Fleabag said, sheepishly. "As you know, dogs find it difficult to hold a grudge. It's just not in our nature. Besides, I doubt you woke up the other morning and said 'Gee, I'd like the fate of a hundred cats placed in my paws because I've nothing better to do today.' I mean, that's not what you said. Right?"

"Right. I didn't say that. My paws are too small to hold a tick, much less the fate of a hundred cats. I never asked for this to happen."

A seagull flew overheard, squawking in disapproval of the dogs taking up the entire beach. Harry looked up at the bird. And then he saw the sky the way Anastasia saw it; filled with clouds and a glorious sun and birds. More importantly, he saw the freedom she yearned for.

Perhaps dogs did have it better than cats, living up on the surface, he thought. Still, whatever had forced the cats to live underground, it wasn't Harry's doing. And yet he couldn't help feeling sorry for them.

"I never asked for this to happen," he said again, though Fleabag and Junior were facing the crowd.

A murmur swept through the crowd, then a hush. The dogs on the beach parted, and Grizzly, Diesel, and Chain strode purposefully toward the jetty.

"Time's up, Harry," Grizzly snarled. "Are you ready to deal?"

"I'd hardly call it a fair trade," Harry said. "You get what you want, and I get nothing I want. How do I even know you'll keep your word and leave Little Rover alone?"

"Dogs always tell the truth."

This was what Harry had told Anastasia. And it was true. Dogs found it impossible to lie. It was more than Dog Law; it was quite impossible for a dog to tell a lie without looking guilty. If a plant was dug up, one guilty look and a dirty snout told you which dog did it. If an expensive cushion was torn to shreds, one awkward look (and usually a few strands of cotton in the mouth) gave up the culprit.

But Harry had also told Anastasia that an omission of the truth was *not* the same as a lie. He was wrong.

Harry looked at the dogs, his friends and his non-friends, and he realised that they deserved to know the truth.

"I kept a secret from you," Harry said in a loud voice. "I know it was wrong to do so, but I wanted to investigate the matter first. I realise now I should have told you right away."

Murmurs rose up from the crowd: *"What secrets?" "A mystery, did he say?" "Harry keeping a secret from us?"*

"It was a big secret too," Harry continued. "It affected every dog in Dog Town, and I kept it to myself. Well, I told Junior and Fleabag and they wanted to tell you, but I asked them not to."

If Harry had listened to Junior and his ominous warnings, he would never have trespassed into Big Rover. He would never have found Cat World. And he would be doing *anything* other than facing the daunting task of telling the dogs about their puppy teeth.

Then he spied Anastasia, waving to him from the top of a kiosk. She had told Harry that Grizzly would find Cat World eventually. Grizzly would, he was a determined dog. And if everything happened for a reason, as Harry often believed, then there had to be an explanation for cats living underground. Grizzly would never stop to find out the reason, being the kind of dog who trashed first and didn't even care to ask questions later.

Once again, the fate of Cat World rested in

Harry's tiny paws. He pitied the cats to have been saddled with him as their saviour.

What a dilemma this was turning out to be. To save the cats, he would hurt his friends. To save his friends, he would hurt the cats. The big dogs seemed to be the only winners in this situation.

In the end, Harry decided that the truth was the real champion. His friends might not like to hear it, but they deserved to know.

He cleared his throat. "I found Cat World, and Grizzly wants me to tell him where it is so he can destroy it. If I refuse, he'll take his anger out on Little Rover instead."

Harry waited for the booing and howling from the small dogs to die down.

In contrast, the big dogs cheered: *"Bring it on." "I haven't had a good rumble in a while."*

Harry was determined to do everything in his power to make sure the big dogs were robbed of the chance to wreak havoc. Except that he had no idea how he was supposed to do this.

Questions came from the crowd:

"Why won't you tell Grizzly where it is?"

"Why does Grizzly want to destroy Cat

World?"

"What proof do you have that cats are real?"

Harry looked at his friends for inspiration. Thankfully Junior and Fleabag were smiling their encouragement. And Anastasia was giving him the thumbs up sign.

Harry lifted his paws to silence the crowd. "I'm afraid there is more news. Something far, far worse than finding Cat World. Grizzly wants to demolish Cat World because—"

"Stop this nonsense," a voice in the crowd barked. "Stop this nonsense at once."

The dog spoke with authority, and all the dogs, big and small, were instantly quiet. Then the wall of dogs parted, allowing Old Roger a clear passage to the jetty.

Old Roger was out of breath by the time he got there.

"Cat World is a place conjured up by a big dog with nothing better to do," Old Roger said. "Leave here this instant, Grizzly. Go home and stop trespassing. The same goes for the small dogs. Stop breaking Dog Law and cease this search for cats."

Grizzly skulked up to the jetty, with Chain

and Diesel a few feet behind.

"I don't care why you have a fascination with wanting to protect them," Grizzly said, "but I want my teeth back and I'm going to get them."

"Teeth?" a dog in the crowd asked. *"What teeth?"*

Old Roger thumped the ground with a stick. "You're talking gibberish. Stop telling fairy tales this instant."

Grizzly snarled. "I'm telling the truth, old dog."

By now, Grizzly had made it to the jetty and he towered over the small dogs.

"The cats have our puppy teeth," he said to the crowd. "And I plan to get them back."

"I plan to get them back too." Harry had to shout to be heard over the noise of the dogs. "I plan to do it peacefully."

More boos and growls came from the dogs.

"Grizzly wants to kill the cats," Harry shouted. "And we've only just found them." He turned a pleading face toward Grizzly. "I need more time to find out what's going on. There has to be a reason why they have our teeth."

Harry felt sure Anastasia would help him solve this mystery, and he was certain she'd help him get their teeth back too. Helping him get the teeth back would be compensation for his helping her get out of her prison.

"How can the cats have our teeth," Old Roger asked, stubbornly, "if cats are a figment of our imagination?"

The tension grew amongst the dogs, creating a rush of adrenalin. This power surge acted like an ON switch for Harry. Suddenly he thought of a way to buy more time.

"How about we race for it," he told Grizzly. "The winner decides the fate."

Grizzly shook his head. "No more games, Harry. You promised you'd tell me at noon. It's now ten minutes past."

"What makes you think I'm playing games?"

"Because you replaced my ultimatum with one of your own," Grizzly said.

"You're just scared I'll beat you."

The crowd of dogs started to laugh. Harry could see Grizzly's lips pulling back into a sneer.

Harry stood on his hind legs to appear as tall as he could.

"What's the bet I win?" Harry cried out.

Old Roger banged his stick on the ground once more. "Betting is against the law, especially on something as stupid as this. I forbid you to carry this obsession any further."

Harry wanted to listen to Old Roger, who was a dog of high authority, but hundreds of cats' lives were in jeopardy.

He would have to disobey Dog Law if he was going to save the cats.

"If you win," Harry told Grizzly. "I'll tell you how to find Cat World. No more stalling, I promise. But if I win, then you have to back off and leave the tooth retrieval to me."

The grin that settled on Grizzly's face caused a chill in Harry. While Harry was the fastest dog in Little Rover, Grizzly was the fastest dog in *all* of Dog Town.

Harry's competitiveness had blinded him to this fact. There was no way he could beat Grizzly. But he had to try.

"You got gumption," Grizzly said with a chuckle. "I'll give you that. You'll only be making a fool of yourself, though."

"I think you're afraid I might actually beat you," Harry said with as much courage as he could muster.

Grizzly laughed those deep, tummy jiggling belly laughs that exposed his canine teeth. Diesel and Chain joined in. Then one by one every other dog joined in, even the small dogs. Except for Old Roger, who had already thrown his stick on the ground and was now heading home.

Almost one hundred dogs were rolling on the ground. It took a long while for the noise to die down.

When it was quiet once more, Grizzly said, "Okay, Harry, if you insist. I accept this challenge."

"Good. I propose we race around the streets of Little Rover."

Harry knew every bump in the road and every angle of every corner. He knew to keep to the left on Sit Boy Lane where the wind was blocked by a delivery truck that never seemed to deliver anything. He knew to slow down at the bottom of Mongrel Street, to give his legs the strength to make it to Fifi Street. And once he was at the top of Fifi Street it was a walk in the park along the downhill stretch of Good Girl Avenue. Then off to a clean finish at the clock tower.

A surge of confidence gushed over him.

I might *actually* win, he thought.

Junior tugged at Harry's ear, and with his paw he beckoned his friend to come closer.

"Have you got distemper?" Junior asked. "Rabies perhaps? Is a tick maybe affecting the way you think?"

"Relax. I know what I'm doing."

"On the contrary, my good friend. Grizzly is the fastest dog on the planet. He can outrun a tornado. Two strides and he'll have lapped you."

"In case you failed to notice," Fleabag said. "Grizzly has really long legs."

"Okay, maybe I forgot about his extra long legs," Harry whispered back. "But I have to do what I can to stop Grizzly waltzing into Cat World and smashing it to pieces. I can beat him, I know it."

"In a lap-sitting contest maybe," Junior said. "But if you're convinced of this, then Fleabag and I are behind you."

"The conference is over," Grizzly shouted. He wore a smug look on his dark face. "Racing around Little Rover will be like taking food from a picnic blanket. How about we make this contest more interesting?"

"How so?" Harry asked.

"What about a swimming contest? You can swim, can't you, shark bait?"

Most dogs disliked baths, but Harry physically feared them. He was pretty sure that swimming was something he would be very, very bad at. Even now, the thought of water made him woozy.

"We compete tomorrow in the Dog Paddle Challenge," Grizzly said. "That's my final offer. Take it or leave it."

Grizzly had held the top position in the Dog Paddle Challenge for three consecutive years. Not only that, it was forbidden for small dogs to enter the prestigious race. And it was a well-known fact that Harry suffered from a fear of water known as ablutophobia.

Yet, despite these damaging odds, Harry agreed to the challenge.

Chapter 25

THE COUNCIL IS NOW IN SESSION

CAT WORLD was run by a leadership committee. At first, when the cats had become detached from the surface, they had tried to live without rules, but that meant nothing was done about food or cleaning. So they set up a committee to make sure the food and cleaning were taken care of.

The committee consisted of six cats: Montgomery, Beauregard, Anastasia, Philippe, Humphrey, and Felicity Anne.

Around a table sat five of the six members. Beauregard was unwell and resting. (If the old cat's complaints were a true indication to his condition, he was on the last of his nine lives.)

News of the challenge between the dogs spread quickly to this committee, who also handled important matters such as what to do if a dog ever discovered their secret city.

"Harry is insane to have accepted the challenge to race in the Dog Paddle Challenge," Philippe announced. "We all know he loathes water."

"He's doomed Cat World," Humphrey said.

"I'd like to know how it is that dogs can decide the fate of cats," Felicity Anne said. "What right have *they* to choose how *we* live?"

Humphrey's tail was swishing madly. "Furthermore, it's absolutely ridiculously preposterous that they want their teeth returned. Those teeth are ours to do with as we see fit. We saw fit to turn them into a statue."

Felicity Anne delicately patted her paw on the table, a sign of her agreement. "Cats were granted Dog Town's puppy teeth. The matter was settled long before Harry interfered."

"Here, here," Philippe and Humphrey muttered simultaneously.

"We must do something about stopping this race," Felicity Anne said.

***

MONTGOMERY had been sitting in silence at the head of the table while the cats bickered. Now he felt the cats' attention turn to him. He slowly turned his head to the side to stare at the easel set up in the corner of the council meeting room.

On the easel was a sheet of cardboard that had an odd-looking diagram drawn on it. He watched in glee as the cats switched their hopeful and bewildered faces between him and the easel.

Montgomery had a plan, but he was remaining tight-lipped about it until the other members had finished their ranting and raving, which seemed to be taking forever.

"If Harry loses, he'll be honour-bound to tell Grizzly about the entrance he found," Philippe said.

Montgomery finally spoke.

"What if Harry wins?" he asked.

"That mutt has about as much chance of winning as I have of growing wings," Humphrey said.

"Quite right. He'll never win on his own." Montgomery paused, expecting a response. When no reply was forthcoming, he drummed his claw on the table. "I said, *he'll never win on his own.*"

"He'll need our help to win," Felicity Anne said, taking the bait and jumping to her feet. Then she hastily sat back down again. "But how do we help him win *and* play games at the same time?"

"Some of us will have to give up recreational activities for this task," Montgomery said.

The committee members, who were usually very talkative, went deathly quiet.

Anastasia broke the silence.

"Would it be such a bad thing if Harry lost?" she asked.

Montgomery stared at her. Then he mimicked her high-pitched voice. "*Would it be such a bad thing if Harry lost*? Of course, it would be a bad thing if Harry lost. Those dogs will come in and destroy our home."

Anastasia swished her tail. "Maybe it's time we returned to the surface."

"All opposed to returning to the surface raise their paws," Montgomery said.

There were eight raised paws. All except Anastasia's.

"You're outnumbered eight to two," Montgomery said. "Now, let's continue with my plan. Harry will need our help if he's to win. Here's what I propose."

Montgomery leapt up and moved over to the easel. As he outlined his plan, the drawing on the piece of cardboard became obvious. When the cats understood the plan, they cheered. Montgomery called it a unanimous win. (Anastasia's opposing view was not recorded)

It was agreed that work was to begin immediately. Montgomery called the meeting adjourned by flicking a bell with his claw.

The bell had once belonged to a cat collar. It was now nailed to the wall, the collar long ago discarded. During the time of their mass departure from the surface, the cats had discarded their collars. And they had banned other things too. Like brushing, claw clipping, baths, curfews, and generally anything that resembled a rule. It was this freedom that Montgomery was devoted to protecting. It was imperative that the liberating life they led in Cat World remained unchanged. At any cost.

He watched Anastasia heave a hopeless sigh as the other committee members ran off to plop themselves in front of the TV. And then he watched her sneak away. Montgomery knew where she was headed. Straight to tell Beauregard of his decision.

He would need to keep an eye on her, he told himself. Because while Montgomery wanted Harry to win, it was clear that Anastasia wanted Harry to lose.

And that was something that could never happen.

Chapter 26

MAKING PLANS

DOG TOWN was abuzz with energy. The big dogs followed Grizzly back to their side of the border. They growled and barked and salivated and were plainly peeved that the fight they'd been promised had been postponed. Thankfully Big Rover was filled with other things to chew on, such as tyres, mattresses, and metal car parts.

Old Roger hurried home so he could lie down to rest. The altercation had exhausted him, and he was a little upset that his words had been left blowing in the wind like forgotten laundry. If the dogs wanted to fight, let them, he decided. He was staying out of it.

The small dogs had rushed home to pack. There were plenty of other towns they could flee to. They'd find new homes and sad-look their way inside. Maybe they'd find a place without big dogs at all.

Harry, Junior, and Fleabag raced back to Harry's kennel.

***

HARRY paced inside his kennel. "We've got to come up with a plan."

"I thought you had a plan," Junior cried. "Why else would you agree to Grizzly's challenge if you had *no plan*?"

"I couldn't help myself," Harry answered. "Still, I know I can beat him, I just need a really good plan."

"You need to learn how to fly," Junior said. "You're forgetting this is a race *in the water*."

"I haven't forgotten," Harry muttered.

"I still don't understand why you want to

protect the cats."

"They stole our puppy teeth, Harry," Fleabag reminded him. "Grizzly has every right to want them back. And, although I have yet to conduct a survey to confirm this, I reckon most of the dogs want them back too."

Junior nodded. "The other dogs won't have a soft spot for cats the way you do."

They were right, of course. Harry had seen the looks of hurt and anger in every single dog when he'd told them about the teeth.

"I have a soft spot for one cat," Harry said. "Her name is Anastasia. I think she is the cat in my dreams. I met her a long time ago."

"How is that possible?" Junior asked. "You only discovered Cat World a day ago."

"When I was a pup, I got lost and found myself in Big Rover. The sky grew dark very quickly."

Harry shivered, remembering the feeling of being lost, cold, and hungry. The memory bubbled to the surface. Clearer than his dreams.

"Go on, Harry," Fleabag urged. "Tell us what happened."

"I was lost and petrified the big dogs would find me. I'd heard such horrible stories about things they did to small dogs trespassing on their land. And I was near the wild forest. Every rustle of the wind sounded like a snake coming to eat me."

Junior and Fleabag huddled in close together.

"Luckily, I was rescued by a black cat," Harry said. "I think it was Anastasia. She played with me until I stopped being scared. But then it started to rain."

Fleabag put her paw to her lips. "Stop, Harry. The suspense is killing me."

"Anastasia took me to a place where I could hide until the rain passed. That place was Cat World. We hid under a cardboard box and we had the best time telling stories and watching the cats do all kinds of silly stuff. They were amazing to watch. Feisty. Creative. Risk-takers. Rule-breakers. Everything we're not. Anyway, Anastasia kept me company and showed me how to get home."

"Wow," Junior said. "You were very lucky. Not many lost pups make it back home."

"I didn't, which is why I repressed the memory of that day," Harry said with a sob. "It was the day I was taken to the pound."

Fleabag wrapped her arms around Harry's neck. "But you found a home, Harry. A lovely home. And I'm glad you did. Otherwise we'd never have become best friends."

Junior nodded. "And best friends stick together. Okay, Harry, we'll help you."

Chapter 27

A DOG-NAPPING

MONTGOMERY waited until twilight, then he tipped a double dose of his sleeping potion into Harry's food bowl. He and the other cats in the dog-napping team then waited for the dog to drop off into a deep sleep. For good measure, Montgomery also hit Harry over the head with a stale bread stick. Lastly, a piece of cloth was tied over the dog's eyes and he was strapped into a little red wagon.

In a hurry to avoid detection, the gang of

four masked cats bolted down the dark alley. They pulled their wagon, with Harry's limp body inside, until the wheels wobbled.

But they didn't slow down until they reached the tunnel's entrance.

"Is all this really necessary?" Felicity Anne asked, panting from all that running. "He already knows how to get into Cat World."

Montgomery gave her a sharp look. "Doesn't *anybody* understand that underestimating these dogs is harmful to our health?"

"Dogs are stupid," she said. "Especially this one. He has allowed himself to be dog-napped twice now."

"Yes, he ought to be *very* embarrassed in the morning," Montgomery said with a sinister chuckle.

The cats towed their captive along the tunnel. This one was located right inside Little Rover not far from the clock tower in the town square. (Harry and Grizzly believed there was only one entrance into Cat World, but there were dozens, which was how the cats had come to deduce that dogs were of lesser intelligence than them.)

"Dogs are stupid," Montgomery agreed. "But they are also cunning. They can lull the unsuspecting fool into a false sense of innocence with what is known as sad-look. Many a ruined shoe has been forgiven because of this look. That's why the blindfold is necessary. You too could fall prey to his wily ways."

It was a bumpy ride across metal grates that ran the length of three houses. But the sleeping potion held up. Harry was still out cold when they arrived in Cat World.

"Wake him up," Montgomery ordered.

Humphrey was holding a mug of cold water. Montgomery knew of Harry's fear of water, so he quickly swiped out a paw.

"Careful," he cried out. "We want to scare the dog, but not to death."

Instead, smelling salts were waved beneath Harry's snout.

Harry came to in an ungainly way, flailing his legs all over the place. "Where am I? What's going on? Help. I'm blind."

When the blindfold was pulled away, Montgomery plastered a Cheshire grin on his face. "Surprise."

"You could have said you wanted to meet me," Harry said, his dark scowl indicating that being dog-napped and tied up was a little over the top. "I'd have come alone."

"True. But this way is much more entertaining." Montgomery stood tall and lifted his chin. "You know something, I think I like this entertainment business. I might set up a theatre. I could do the choreography and the music."

"Please, no more singing," Harry said. "I'll do anything you want. Just don't sing."

Montgomery feigned regret. "Sorry, but I've been practicing all day while working in my secret laboratory. Your objection is overruled."

He whipped a harmonica up to his lips and blew a single note. As one, the cats burst into song:

Clever and pretty and always on guard
Free to be free and not fenced in a yard
Able to stay out all night and have fun
If you could be a cat, you would be one

Curfews and collars and clippings are banned

Life in Cat World is positively grand
Who needs to see rain, stars, or the sun?
If you could be a cat, you would be one

Fur that is fluffy and soft to the touch
Patting and petting we crave not so much
Unlike you dogs who pine when you've none
If you could be a cat, you would be one

Choosy with whom we become friendly with
While each other's bottoms, dogs sniff and sniff
Who knows where that dog has put his bum
If you could be a cat, you would be one

If you only knew how much better it was
Dancing and singing, and much more, because
We know how to live life and how to have fun
If you could be a cat, you would be one

The song ended. Harry had his paws against his ears.

"Cats sing an awful lot," he said. "And they do it rather loudly."

"Yes, I am *truly* surprised we've gone undiscovered for as long as we have,"

Montgomery said. "I'm curious, what songs do dogs sing?"

"None that I know of." Harry suddenly brightened. "Oh, I know a poem."

(It was, in fact, the only poem Harry knew, and the poem he sometimes repeated over and over to put himself to sleep on sleepless nights.)

Montgomery clapped his hands in glee. "Lovely. Let's hear it."

Harry sat on his haunches and sang:

A B C D E F G
Food, Play, Sleep, Dig, Chew, Run, Wee
H I J K L M N
Food, Play, Sleep, then do it all again
A B C D E F G
Food, Play, Sleep, Dig, Chew, Run, Wee

"Is that it?" Montgomery asked. "What happened to the rest of the alphabet?"

Harry shrugged his shoulders. "What's an alphabet?"

Montgomery's furry ears twitched. "The letters used in writing a language."

"You must come from another planet," Harry scoffed. "Because where I come from animals are neither readers nor writers."

"*This* is why cats are higher up the evolutionary ladder than dogs," Montgomery shouted. "Even if dogs were to catch up, we would always surpass their level of intelligence simply because cats know better than to let a reindeer hat be placed on its head. Anyway, as to why you're here, Harry. Let's not wait another minute."

Montgomery clapped his hands in a brusque manner, and a door opened. Through this door was a device, draped in a white sheet. Four cats wheeled it into the chamber.

A second sheet-covered object followed. Then another, and another, until there were five sheet-covered contraptions crammed into the room. The cats eyed the concealed objects with greed, and their tails quivered in pleasure.

Montgomery said in a loud voice, "It has come to our attention that you are to race Grizzly in the Dog Paddle Challenge. It is a race you are bound to lose."

"Is there nobody who has faith in me?" Harry asked.

"The odds are against you even finishing the race, Harry. But with our help, you can win. And you must."

Montgomery lifted his paws high in the air. "Behold. My magnificent instruments of defeat."

The sheet was whisked away.

Everyone gasped. Beneath the sheet was a glass contraption in the shape of a fish.

Chapter 28

MAKING ALLIES

ANASTASIA wasn't at the unveiling of the giant fish. She had seen the plans and they had terrified her. She had gone to speak to her father to see if he could knock some sense into Montgomery.

She found Beauregard where he'd been for the past two weeks, in bed with a blanket pulled up to his chin.

"So what ingenious plan has Montgomery come up with to make sure Harry wins?" he asked Anastasia when she came to visit.

"It's unbelievable. You'll have to see it to believe it." She shook her head and gave a snort. "It's downright crazy."

"But will it work?"

"Montgomery is a determined cat. He's already read dozens of self-help manuals. That alone is bound to make his plan succeed. But it's too risky. For everyone involved."

"Go to Harry," Beauregard said. "You are right, my wise daughter. Tell Harry that there are cats who want him to lose this race. Tell him to stop this nonsense and let Grizzly know how to find us. I've little time left on this earth to see the sun."

Beauregard gave a succession of weak coughs which Anastasia knew were for effect.

"Oh, hush," she said. "It's just a cold."

She was determined to see her father enjoy a few more years yet, but not here. Up on the surface. She wanted to take him there, right away if possible. But there was still the question of where they'd live.

"I still need to find a safe place," she said. "I've seen a couple of houses I like the look of. But dogs live there already."

"There was a time when dogs and cats lived together in harmony, you know," Beauregard said.

"I know, Father. You've told me the legend. But I'd prefer to find a house without a dog. I have discovered that dogs go potty all over the place. On the lawn, on the garden, on the trees, on the pavement." She swished her tail. "They go wherever they feel like it. It's unsanitary."

"That's because they've had too many years with somebody else picking up after them. If they had to do it themselves, I suspect they'd understand the benefit of toileting in a hygienic box."

"I shouldn't have to train them. They should already be trained."

Beauregard patted his daughter's paw. "My dear girl, I'm certain our new home will be perfect as long as we're together."

He closed his eyes. Anastasia studied his face as a smile played on his lips.

"What are you thinking about, Father?" she asked.

"I'm thinking that it will be nice to feel the sun again. I do miss it."

"You'll have plenty of time to laze about in the sun soon enough." Anastasia fluffed his pillow and gathered up his empty milk bowl for washing. "I suppose the dogs will be happy to get their teeth back. Hopefully when they're happy, they'll be more open to the idea of cats living amongst them."

Beauregard frowned. "The sooner they get their teeth back the better. I detest that ghastly statue."

Chapter 29

A TREACHERY

MONTGOMERY stared with pride at his devices. The giant fish had see-through walls. They had a tail and fins and big eyes. Inside the see-through fish was a bicyclc, and it was attached to ropes and strings and a periscope.

Inside the closest giant fish were Harry's best friends, Junior and Fleabag.

Even though the dogs banged their paws against the walls, they couldn't be heard. Because the walls were soundproof.

"Let them go," Harry growled at Montgomery. "Or I swear I'll go outside right now and yap my head off until Grizzly finds you."

"You are hardly in the position to be making demands. I will let your friends go when the race is over. In the meantime, they are my insurance that you will do as you are told."

"What am I supposed to be doing exactly?" Harry asked.

"When the race starts, you will jump into the water at Buster Bay along with all the other dogs. Then you will swim for the jetty. We cats will use these fish devices to sabotage the race from beneath the surface."

"Sabotage?" Harry asked.

"I will help you win the race."

"I know what sabotage means. How will you help me win?"

Montgomery pointed to a cat who wore bright yellow goggles, a mask, and a snorkel on his head. The underwater-geared cat then hopped inside one of the fish devices and started peddling, moving the fish tail from left to right, demonstrating the mechanics of the machine. The large hall of cats cheered and applauded.

Montgomery raised a hand and the cat inside the giant fish pushed a button. The fisheyes extended out and turned into grabbing claws. The claws clutched the air.

"That device will latch onto the legs of the big dogs," Montgomery said. "Thus preventing them from competing in the race."

Harry's eyes went wide. "They'll drown."

"A minor technicality," Montgomery said with a wave of his white paw. "In battle, casualties are to be expected."

"Excuse me, Montgomery." Humphrey pushed his way through the crowd of onlookers. "Wait just one minute. Did I hear you say these things will be *under water*? Who are you expecting to operate these giant fish?"

"Cats will operate them, of course," Montgomery said.

"But cats don't like water. We like water less than Harry."

"Another minor technicality. Sacrifices are to be made." Montgomery addressed the crowd. "I need three cats to volunteer. You shall have a statue made in your honour."

"Noooo." Harry was barking, and this

caused the cats to hiss and spit. "The dogs will drown. You can't do this."

Montgomery lifted a paw and the cats went quiet.

"I *can* do this. And I am."

"You're despicable," Harry cried. "First you stole our teeth, and now you want to kill the big dogs."

Montgomery smiled. "My little friend. You are mistaken if you think we steal your teeth. They were bequeathed to us."

"I doubt any dog would dare give his puppy teeth away. And I'm sure the Tooth Fairy has something to say about it as well."

"I see you need proof." Montgomery thumped the ground with his paw and his voice boomed inside the chamber. "Bring me the scroll!"

Bangs and clangs echoed inside the chamber. Finally, a cat emerged and placed a rolled-up scroll in Montgomery's paws. As carefully as if it were made from porcupine's needles, he unrolled the document.

"It is a good thing that cats can read," he said, slipping on a pair of wire-rimmed glasses. "I always suspected it would come to this. That's why I kept this scroll hidden safely away. You dogs are devious creatures." Montgomery sighed heavily. "I've said this again and again, yet nobody listens."

"Just get on with it," Harry said. "The race will be over by the time you've finished moaning."

"Very well." Montgomery cleared his throat. "From this day forth, small dogs will reside in the south of Dog Town, to be henceforth known as Little Rover. Big dogs will reside in the north of Dog Town, to be henceforth know as Big Rover. And all cats will reside in the hidden underworld, to be henceforth known as Cat World. As compensation for this exile, the cats will be granted the puppy teeth of big and small dogs. And they shall do with these teeth whatever they please. Signed, Shan of Big Rover, Old Roger of Little Rover, and Beauregard of Cat World."

Montgomery thrust the document in Harry's face.

"I can't read," Harry said.

"But you recognize the paw print of Old Roger?"

Harry nodded. "That is Old Roger's paw print. But why would he do this to us dogs?"

"Perhaps you should ask him yourself. Another time."

Montgomery rolled up the scroll and handed it to another cat. Then he snapped a set of goggles on his head.

"I'm afraid you've taken such a long time to rouse from the sleeping potion that half the day has gone. The race starts in one hour."

Montgomery and a handful of cats swished their way toward the giant fish.

"Oh, and Harry." Montgomery had stopped at top of the ladder leading into his giant fish. "You better not be thinking about sabotaging *my* plan. Or your friends will be collecting barnacles at the bottom of Buster Bay along with the big dogs."

Montgomery climbed inside his fish.

***

HARRY couldn't stop his heartbeat from racing as he watched dozens of cats push the giant fish contraptions along the floor. Another group of cats pulled on a rope that opened a door previously concealed behind a bamboo blind. Daylight seeped in through the gap.

Harry could see all the way across to the jetty, where hundreds of dogs were gathered on the shore of Buster Bay, ready for the Dog Paddle Challenge.

How many times had Harry gazed up at this rocky outcrop and been spooked by it, never knowing it formed part of Cat World. But if cats lived in this rocky outcrop, then Cat World didn't just exist underground. It existed in every hidden nook and cranny, high and low. The cats had, in effect, lived right under the noses of dogs.

The grind of the wheels against the concrete floor captured Harry's attention. He watched the fish devices, manned by cats in snorkels and goggles, get wheeled out onto the cliff. They were lifted high into the air by more ropes and pulleys. The fish devices were carried by rope across the rocky outcrop and toward the waterline.

By now, cats had positioned themselves around Fleabag and Junior's cone of captivity, releasing their sharp claws and waving them like knives.

A cat untied Harry and aimed a water pistol at him.

"You can go now," the cat said. "And you had better do as Montgomery says. Leave the sabotaging to us. We'll make sure you win the race."

"I can't leave my friends behind," Harry said.

Fleabag and Junior were still inside their fish device, banging on the wall. They were barking, although Harry couldn't hear a thing.

And they couldn't hear Harry, but he got the impression they knew exactly what was going on, because Fleabag blew him a kiss and pointed to the cave entrance.

She mouthed the single word, "Go."

Harry looked at Junior, his good friend who could always talk sense into any dog.

Junior nodded. He mouthed one word: "Win."

A sickening feeling filled Harry about leaving his friends behind. That sickening feeling turned to mortifying dread at the thought of jumping into the water at Buster Bay and competing in a race he now knew he could never win.

All this trouble just to save these cats.

These cats were despicable, he thought. They didn't deserve his help.

And then he spied Anastasia, who was huddled up with a group of cats. They looked as frightened as Harry felt. These cats didn't want to be locked up in Cat World anymore. These cats wanted to be free to roam the surface, to feel the sun, to watch the stars.

Harry took a deep breath, then he bolted for the doorway Montgomery and his fiendish cats had taken.

He scampered down the cliff to the shoreline below.

Chapter 30

BURIED IN THE PAST

OLD ROGER lay fast asleep in a basket beside a window. Stretched out flat, he twitched in his sleep as though dreaming. He *was* dreaming, about a time when he was young, and not the dog he was now: nearly blind, toothless, and practically furless. At least he still attracted the lady dogs. (Because he was also half deaf he was known amongst the females as a good listener).

A clock chimed somewhere in the house,

startling Old Roger.

"Darn that pesky clock. And darn those pesky dogs for ruining my sleep."

But Old Roger's sleep had been broken long before Harry and his friends had shown up claiming to have found Cat World. So the old dog got up.

Slowly, he pushed through the flap on the back door and followed the path until he came to the clothesline. There, he crossed the recently mowed grass and headed to the flowering hydrangea bush.

He stopped to take in the scent of the mauve flowers and make a wish to be young again. Then he pushed headfirst through the shrubbery.

Buried in the furthest corner of Old Roger's backyard was his beloved treasure trove. The collection was started the day he moved into this yard. Ever since then he'd added new mementos as they'd come to him.

Like the squeaky rubber toy his very first girlfriend had given him, the one that had lost its squeak but not its sentiment.

And then there was the bright-red heart-shaped dog tag from a visiting lady Chihuahua.

Because he'd captured her heart, she'd said.

Buried here was also the last bone the Furless Ones had given him before his teeth had fallen out.

Now Old Roger scratched at the dirt. He scratched until he uncovered the most precious thing in his hiding spot.

There, poking up through the dirt and looking like the tip of a bean sprout, was one of Old Roger's puppy teeth. It was the last remaining puppy tooth in all of Dog Town.

The cats had the rest.

But they were not the thieves that Grizzly and Harry believed them to be.

Old Roger carried the tooth to his basket. He felt bad for lying to the dogs gathered at the jetty (especially since he'd help write Dog Law) but the truth was even more damaging.

He stared at the tooth, waiting for it to give him a sign. When no sign was forthcoming, he took this as his sign to do nothing.

So Old Roger did exactly that – nothing. He nestled into his basket and went back to sleep.

Chapter 31

THE FIRST STONE

BEAUREGARD slipped out of his bedroom and tiptoed through the big concrete chamber of Cat World. At the archway, he gave a quick glance in each direction to make sure his aging cat senses were working. They were. Nobody was following him.

He stepped into the tunnel, walking as fast as he could without rattling the three jade stones stashed in a bag around his neck. These were different than regular stones. These were communication devices.

He stroked the smooth surfaces, closing his eyes, hoping they still worked. It had been a long, long time since he'd last lain eyes on these, believing them to be lost.

He had spent the good part of an hour looking for them. He was very displeased to discover that Montgomery had been using them as eyes for his hideous statue. Beauregard's old bones had struggled with the climb up the statue, but he'd made it to the top and removed the jade stones.

He'd made it undetected to the tunnel that Harry had found.

Now, up on the surface that had been denied to Beauregard for all these years, it took him a moment to adjust his eyes against the bright glare of the sun.

"How I have missed you," he whispered, letting the warm rays caress his fur.

The breeze tickled his whiskers. The air smelled empty, as though the overpowering aromas in Cat World had robbed him of his sense of smell. But after a brief moment, the gentlest, faintest, lightest whiff of the ocean delighted his nostrils.

"I have missed a great many things," he said. "But I have no time to dwell on them now. I must hurry."

Beauregard looked left toward Big Rover, then right toward Little Rover. Whichever order he visited the homes of the Dog Town elders was trivial. What mattered was that they remember the meaning of the jade stones.

The fate of all cat-kind depended on it.

Chapter 32

THE SECOND STONE

OLD ROGER took a lot longer to wake up these days. After going to the garden to look at the hidden tooth, he had decided that it offered no insight. It was a tooth and nothing more. So he went back to dreaming. A short while later, something rattled against the window where he slept. The noise did little to rouse him (he *was* half deaf after all). But the need to go outside came upon him.

Despite the chill that attacked his furless

body whenever he went outdoors, he obliged his bladder by taking it outside.

When he arrived at his favourite potty spot in the garden, a bare patch beneath the window, he stepped on a smooth stone. He looked at the rock. It was shiny and green. He'd never seen this sort of rock in his garden bed before.

He stared at it for a very long time. It was a jade stone, but the meaning of the stone eluded him.

He continued to stare at it, trying to decide if this green stone should bother him or not.

Old Roger finally gave up staring at the rock (outstaring a rock is a difficult thing to do), and he went back inside the house to sleep.

He quickly forgot all about the jade stone.

But Old Roger was an elderly dog. As for his toilet habits, he had come full circle in life. He had a bladder like a pup and needed to go to the toilet every few minutes.

Old Roger made his way once more around the garden to his favourite potty spot. Here, beneath the window where he slept, the garden bed was devoid of flowers that grew in abundance throughout the rest of the garden. After a few mandatory sniffs, Old Roger stepped on something hard. He looked down and wondered if he should be bothered by the smooth green stone or not. He'd never seen a rock such as this in his garden bed before.

"Curse my fading memory," Old Roger growled. "But this rock does ring a bell. Why would someone give me a jade stone? It must have some meaning to it."

He started muttering to himself to jog his memory.

"Jade, jade, jade. I wonder what that particular stone represents."

Then it dawned on him.

"Oh, no," he said.

Old Roger realised what the stone meant.

It meant trouble.

Chapter 33

THE THIRD STONE

SHAN, the third member in this trio of Elders who had helped create Dog Law, was in another part of Dog Town. She was woken by a small object hitting her on the nose.

"Blast those pups," she yelped.

Then Shan remembered that she was alone in her pen, and the young pups she cursed for biting her tail and ears had grown up and moved out years ago. I miss those days, she told herself. Grizzly had better hurry up and give me grand-pups, she added as an afterthought.

She sat up and saw a green stone at the foot of her bed. But unlike Old Roger, Shan's memory was in tip-top shape. She immediately knew what the green rock meant. And she would have agreed with Old Roger that the stone meant trouble.

Ten minutes later, Shan arrived in the abandoned alley where all this nonsense about dogs and cats had first begun. She saw Beauregard sitting by the door that had once belonged to the butcher shop. The cat looked older, but then she supposed she looked older too. She certainly felt as ancient as an Egyptian mummy.

Beauregard had always been a large grey tabby cat with a wide girth and a chubby face, but old age had made him skinny as a rake. And his fur looked wiry too, like a steel brush, uninviting to touch. Still, his eyes were bright with cunning and intelligence. She knew to be cautious of anything he said.

"It's been a long time, Shan," Beauregard said, his voice full of kindness though still high-pitched as all cats speak. "A long time spent apart because of a silly argument."

Shan blew a quick gust of hot air through her nostrils. "I'm only here because dogs keep their word. I don't regret what happened between us. But I've changed my mind about the puppy teeth. I want them back."

"We used to share the sunshine with dogs," Beauregard said in a wistful tone. "I want those days back."

"Not gonna happen if you don't return our teeth," Shan said rudely.

Old Roger came around the corner. He wore a tartan coat and wheezed like he'd run all the way.

"This has better be worth my while," he said. "It's too cold for me to be outdoors."

"It's summer, Roger," Shan said.

"It might be summer to you. But when you're hairless, winter is an eternal sensation."

"Well, I am glad you both remembered the meaning of the jade stones," Beauregard said. "And I'm doubly impressed you remembered the way to this place."

The place Beauregard referred to was an alley that had once backed onto a string of shops. It had been a long, long time ago when the three Elders had first met. So much had changed, it was a miracle they found their way without getting lost. Yet it hadn't changed too much that it was impossible to picture the alley the way it used to be.

"I'd recognise that faded wooden door anywhere," Old Roger said, gazing longingly at the butcher's door.

"Remember the night we first met. Here in this alley," Beauregard said.

Shan could remember it. Nostalgia sat thick on the air like fog.

"I was scared," Beauregard said.

"Me too," Old Roger whispered.

Shan grunted. "I remember I was sad about being left here on my own, without even a toy. But then I realised I wasn't alone. You two were huddled together in a box. The look on both your faces, well, you seemed sadder than me. So I decided to be strong for all of us."

Old Roger pointed at the butcher's door. "That first night we got sausages from the kind butcher. His cranky wife kept yelling at him to stop feeding us strays, but he was always good to us."

"We came back night after night," Shan said, "even after we'd found nice homes. We pretended we were homeless once a week just to get free sausages."

Beauregard licked his lips. "I miss those sausages. And we never once told another cat or dog who was giving us the free food."

"It was a secret worth keeping," Shan said with a nod.

"I especially liked the chicken sausages," Old Roger said.

Shan frowned. "We never had chicken sausages."

"Oh. Blast my fading memory. Still, I do like chicken sausages."

Beauregard cleared his throat. "I suppose you know why I sent you the jade stones."

"None of it matters anymore," Old Roger said. "I'm too old to stop what's about to happen. Harry is a determined dog."

Shan huffed. "I'd say he's more than determined. He's crazy. Grizzly is the fastest dog in Dog Town."

Beauregard held up a paw. "Sadly, I have to agree that Grizzly is the obvious winner in today's race. And there are many cats that will be glad to see the end of their confinement, myself included. But Grizzly plans on harming us, and I must stop that from happening."

"You're assuming that Harry will lose this race," Old Roger yapped. "I take offence to that. I'll have you know he is the fastest dog in Little Rover. I've seen him outrun a bicycle."

"The winner of this race is the least of my concerns," Beauregard said. "What's important is that Grizzly agrees not to harm the cats when he demolishes Cat World."

Shan felt both their stares. "I won't tell him what to do. He's the leader of Big Rover and he has a right to rule it however he wants. If this is anyone's fault, it's Harry's. He found Cat World and couldn't keep it a secret."

Old Roger shuffled up to her. "I might have a feeble memory, but I'm not stupid. Harry *stumbled* upon Cat World, but I know for a fact that Grizzly has been *searching* for it. I wonder who told him about its existence."

Shan lunged at Beauregard.

"It's your fault," she snarled. "If Montgomery had kept the teeth in a box, instead of making them into a statue of a cat, the dogs would have no reason to be upset."

Beauregard reared back. "How do you know about the statue?"

Shan leered at him. "I overheard one of your cats talking about building a second statue. I thought to myself, a *second* statue? I didn't know they'd built a first. Never would have agreed to this if I'd known you were gonna do *that* to our teeth."

"I didn't do anything," Beauregard said. "It's Montgomery's fault."

Shan huffed. "Well, I'm glad it's come to this, because I've realised it was wrong to grant you the big dogs' teeth. I want ours back."

"Well, if she gets her teeth back, then I want ours back," Old Roger said.

"We will," Shan told him. "Harry has agreed to tell Grizzly how to find Cat World after he loses the Dog Paddle Challenge."

"He may win," Beauregard pointed out.

"Please. He won't," Shan said.

"Harry can win," Old Roger said, his furless face turning purple. "Stop saying Harry has no hope of winning. He can beat Grizzly. I'd bet my life on it."

Shan laughed. "Not gonna happen. It's a well-known fact that Grizzly is the biggest and fastest dog in Dog Town. He's the overall champion of the Dog Paddle Challenge, and has been for the past three years. Small dogs have never competed, and there lies their disadvantage."

"He can win," Old Roger growled.

"Not without help. And I'll stop anyone who helps him. There's only one rule in the Dog Paddle Challenge. The Furless One may accompany their dog, but the dog *must* swim the race."

"He *can* win without help," Old Roger barked. "I say we place a bet on the winner."

Beauregard gave a shrill whistle. It was so shrill that it caused Shan and Old Roger to cover their ears (though not so much Old Roger because he was half deaf).

"Your betting is how this whole fiasco started in the first place," Beauregard said. "You two lost and I ended up underground with a pile of teeth I never wanted. I'll have you know, this is the first time I have felt the sun in a long, long time."

"Has it been that long?" Shan remarked, suddenly ashamed at herself for what the cats had suffered from a moment of fury.

Her fury. The argument that had separated the three friends a long, long time ago had been her doing. And she had neither apologised nor explained her actions, despite wanting to, again and again. But it seemed like she was always raising puppies. Puppies that needed her attention. So the needs of others, including her own, had grown less and less important over the years. And the more time that went by, the wider the gap became, until the gap was so wide, no bridge would have been stable enough to cross it.

"Thankfully, we cats are nocturnal," Beauregard said, snapping her back to the present. "Or I dare say we'd never have coped. And thankfully Dog Law states that dogs must remain off the streets at night, otherwise we'd never have gotten any opportunity to come up for fresh air."

Old Roger lowered his head and his voice was sorrowful. "A long, long time without sunlight is a long, long time. I suppose we should do something about changing it."

Beauregard flicked his tail. "I'm glad you're seeing sense. The smell of that dark place is intolerable. There are so many things I've wanted to do on the surface before I die."

Alarmed, Shan said, "You should have sent

us the green stones sooner."

Beauregard shook his head. "It's not that simple. Montgomery would never dream of giving up his uncontrolled, free-and-easy lifestyle for a chance to live on the surface. I only wish Harry had found us sooner. I wouldn't mind Grizzly and his henchdogs smashing up Cat World. But he must not harm the cats."

Beauregard looked up at the butcher's door. "I remember when I shared a home with a dog. I remember controlled feed times, flea baths and collars, nail clippings and brushing. These things seemed like an anchor around my neck at the time, but now I would give anything to return to that world. I want to feel the sun on my back, to play-fight with a dog, to chase birds. Oh, to chase birds again. But more than anything in the world, I want to curl up into a Furless One's lap. Especially a child's lap. They have so much love to give. I miss being on the receiving end of it."

Shan looked up at the faded wooden door and became swept up in the nostalgic moment.

"Things were simpler when we were homeless," she said with a sigh. "Okay,

Beauregard, I'll do as you ask. I'll tell Grizzly not to harm the cats."

Old Roger chuckled. "If he's anything like his mother, he won't listen."

And that was what Shan was worried about.

Chapter 34

WHERE IT ALL BEGAN

A LONG, LONG TIME AGO, on a chilly morning, three baby animals had been left in the alley behind the old shops. In this alley stood a clothing alteration shop, a video arcade, a chemist, and a butcher shop.

Naturally, the three abandoned animals congregated at the door of the butcher's shop.

The butcher was a kind man who had always wanted pets but had never found the time to look after them. He smiled at the animals and asked them their names. They introduced themselves: Shan, a speckled-brown Great Dane pup; Beauregard, a grey tabby kitten; and Roger, a Miniature Fox Terrier with a white coat that had patches of black and tan all over it.

Thankfully, the butcher was a perfectionist when it came to making his sausages. If a sausage was imperfect in any way, in length, thickness, or shape, he would throw it in the bin outside. But that morning, Shan, Beauregard, and Roger had sat by his back step, drawn there by the warmth ebbing from the crack under the door. The butcher took pity on their cheerless faces and tossed his imperfect sausages to the animals.

This happened for many weeks. The animals had developed such a liking for the sausages and the kind butcher that even after they had found homes, they returned once a week for a pat on the head and a free feed.

Weeks became months and the animals became the best of friends. They grew up. Beauregard was less clumsy. Roger's teeth fell out and new ones appeared. Shan grew into an enormous dog. Roger stayed small enough to fit in a shoe. Yet, they kept coming back for their weekly pat on the head and a free sausage.

They did not particularly like keeping a secret. Animals are rather fond of boasting, however, these sausages were simply too good to share. How they managed to get away with eating these treats without getting caught was a testament to their determination to *not* get caught. Anyway, as time passed, Shan became leader to the big dogs, Roger became the leader of the small dogs, and Beauregard was leader to the cats.

And still they returned each week.

The butcher had a wife who was a cranky woman. And she had an insatiable appetite. She would always get cranky with her husband for giving the imperfect sausages to the strays. In her opinion, the sausages were perfectly fine to eat as they were.

One fine Wednesday morning, like every other Wednesday morning for the past six months, Shan, Roger, and Beauregard stopped by the butcher shop to say hello and enjoy a free sausage. However, on this day, it was not the butcher who opened the door, but his cranky wife.

She threw rocks at them instead of sausages and told them never to come to the alley again. The stones were smooth and green, quite unlike any rock the three animals had ever seen.

"Oh well, we knew it was too good to last forever," Beauregard said, licking the stone.

"They have no taste, but they are pretty," Shan agreed. "We could keep these, one each, as a sign of our alliance. And if we're ever feeling sad or lonely, we can use them to remember the good times we had here."

"I bet I can sneak in," Roger said, who had no interest in the jade stones. He was staring up at a small window that was to the left of the door, located about five feet off the ground.

"How on earth do plan to do that?" Beauregard asked.

He was a cat, and therefore curious about everything. He was very intrigued to know how a dog, without the feline acrobatic skills that he possessed, would manage a five-foot-high leap into the air.

Roger jumped up onto a wooden crate that sat beneath the window. "I'll climb in through here. When the cranky woman throws me out, you two can run inside and snatch up the sausages."

"That's a ridiculous plan," Beauregard said. "What if she locks you inside and turns you into a sausage?"

"She is rather fond of sausages," Shan said with a nod. "It's likely she'll do as Beauregard says. Besides, it's too high up. You'll break a leg, or worse, your neck."

Beauregard was sizing up the window. "Shan is correct. If anyone can get inside, it's a cat." He hopped up on the crate and pushed Roger out of the way. "Cats are far superior at jumping than dogs."

Shan stood up on her hind legs and rested her front paws on the windowsill. "I can easily reach the window."

Beauregard jumped down from the crate. "Yes, you are tall, but you still lack the agility to jump from the ground through the window. But, out of the two of you, I believe you'd stand a better chance of getting inside. Only a slim chance, though."

"Are you saying I'm too small to matter?" Roger growled in an angry tone.

"I think he is," Shan said, chuckling

merrily. "Small dogs are good for petting, but not for doing hard work."

"I can work all day."

"Chasing mice?"

"Argue no more," Beauregard said, bowing to the dogs. "I promise to give you a sausage to share after I claim my prize."

Roger became irate. "I can get in through the window. I'll even bet on it."

"Hah," Shan laughed. "Look who's making bets he'll never keep?"

Shan had said this in mockery, but Roger was sincere when he said, "I'd bet my puppy teeth on it."

Every dog knew that Roger stored his puppy teeth, along with all his other prized possessions, in the garden behind a hydrangea bush. He must have been confident to wager his treasured belongings. But one attempt at getting in through the window turned into twenty. And by the thirtieth jump, Roger had not only lost all his teeth, he'd wagered the puppy teeth of every small dog he knew.

Shan was next to go. Her attempts were just as unsuccessful, and after her twentieth jump at the window (landing with a flinchingly heavy thud every time) she too had lost all of her teeth and those of every big dog she knew.

The two dogs started arguing over whose turn it was to jump next. Beauregard, who had grown tired of listening to their competitive bickering, had slipped inside the butcher shop via a missing tile on the rooftop. Then he'd picked the lock on the back door, strolled through with a string of sausages on his shoulder, and declared himself the winner.

He was a little shocked at the sudden anger the dogs showed toward him. They snarled and growled. Then they called him a cheat.

"I won fur and square," he said, his eyes narrowing and his ears flattening.

"You were supposed to go through the window," Shan barked.

"The bet to jump through the window was between you two. I said I'd get *inside*." Beauregard looked up at the window. "And had either of you cared to look closely, you would have noticed that the window was painted shut.'

"So you did cheat," Shan growled. "You had an unfair advantage when you checked out the window."

Roger's face turned a deep shade of purple. "*And* you sat by and watched us hurt ourselves as we bashed against the window, knowing full well there was no way we'd dislodge it."

Beauregard puffed out his chest. "Dogs are poor losers. You should learn to wear your loss with the grace of a cat."

"You cheated."

"I won."

"Cheated."

"Won."

Shan sat down on her haunches. "He's right. Beauregard is the winner. And Roger and I bet all the puppy teeth to the winner. A dog's word is a promise."

Roger groaned. "A dog's word is a promise. The puppy teeth of the small dogs are yours, Beauregard."

The cat looked aghast. "What am I supposed to do with your stupid teeth? All I wanted was the sausages."

He stroked the string of sausages, holding onto them as if they were as precious as a string of pearls. And to the cat they were invaluable. (What he lovingly held in his paws were the perfect sausages the butcher prided himself on. Therefore it stood to reason that they would taste better than the *imperfect* sausages he and his friends had been sharing for the past six months.)

"If you eat those sausages you'll have to find a new best friend," Roger said, licking his lips. He had applied the same logic as Beauregard that these sausages would taste better.

Beauregard paused mid-stroke. Roger was a bit of a hot-head who often said things he regretted later. Still, he was a good friend. And dogs did lose their sense of humour when it came to food. So Beauregard had to assume that Roger's threat was genuine, and therefore the cat would need to do something to keep the dog's friendship.

Beauregard sliced one of the sausages in half and handed it over to Roger.

"I did say I'd give you a sausage to share," Beauregard said.

Shan swiped at the morsel. It went flying into the air and splattered up against the wall. Three pairs of eyes watched the piece of sausage as it slowly peeled away from the wall and splattered to the ground.

Shan snarled. "If either of you take one bite of those sausages, you'll need to find another new best friend. Give them to me."

"I'll never give them up," Beauregard shrieked. "They're mine, I tell you. Mine." Then he took off running down the alleyway.

Roger and Shan gave chase. The cat was easy to follow: they simply followed the string of sausages. They had almost caught Beauregard, but then he ducked into a stormwater drain.

Growling at the opening, Shan barked ferociously, "If I ever see you or your friends again, I'll tear you apart. You'd better stay down there, Beauregard. Do you hear me? This is Dog Town now."

Then she threw her jade stone at the cat.

"That was a bit harsh," Roger said. "Is banishing our best friend to a life underground really necessary? You'll apologise tomorrow."

Shan, too angry to speak, snatched Roger's jade stone out from his hand and threw it across the road where it landed in the playground.

"Hey, that's my stone," Roger cried. "Get it back for me. This instant."

"I really do object to being told what to do

by a dog that is no bigger than my paw," she said.

Roger stared at Shan, dumbfounded. "What's gotten into you, Shan?"

"Beauregard became my enemy when he cheated. And you'll be next if you keep defending him."

"But Shan, this is silly. This will all blow over in the morning. Just you wait and see."

"He's a cheat and you're a bossy-boots. I'd be better off without the pair of you."

Shan turned around and ran toward home.

The very next day, Beauregard, who was madder than a rodeo bull at Shan's outburst, returned to the surface to draw up the legal document that resulted in the separation of dogs and cats.

It was the last time the three animals saw each other.

Chapter 35

THE DOG PADDLE CHALLENGE

HARRY was reluctant to leave his best friends as prisoners in Cat World, but he had no choice other than to make his way down the ragged rock-face and head to the jetty.

He arrived just as a large wooden boat was sidling up against the wharf. Two Furless Ones jumped off the boat and shouted to each other. Then they grabbed at ropes and lashed them around T-shaped fasteners on the jetty. They shouted at each other once more before jumping back onto the boat.

Twelve large dogs stood in a line, nose to tail, ready to embark. Once on board they would be ferried across to Mystery Island. From there the dogs would swim back to the shore.

The winner of the Dog Paddle Challenge was awarded a basket of tinned food. While this was a much coveted prize, today the dogs fought to win first place for another reason.

(Unbeknown to the Furless Ones, today's winner got to decide the fate of Cat World. They merely thought the large attendance of dogs was due to the glorious weather.)

Harry joined the end of the line. He told himself to keep looking up at the sky as he stepped onto the jetty, but he had to look down or risk falling through the cracks.

The gaps in the jetty were the size of his paws. A few feet below him, green waves gently slapped against the pylons. Thankfully the water was relatively calm and Harry was spared from getting wet by the spray that might otherwise have whooshed up through the gaps.

He pictured his friends being held captive inside the giant fish device, shaking with anger and fright. It was this thought alone that kept him shuffling his way along the line.

"Glad you could make it, shark bait," Grizzly shouted from the front of the queue. "I thought you might have chickened out."

"Fat chance," Harry replied, discovering that lying through his teeth was easy, but it still tasted bitter in his mouth. "I'm looking forward to doing a victory lap around Buster Bay."

"Look at this, Diesel," Chain said, who stood in line behind Grizzly. "I'm not sure I've eaten a drowned dog before."

Diesel smiled. "It'll taste fishy."

The line moved forward once more, inching Harry forward until he came face to face with the boat. He took a deep breath and hopped onto the ferry.

Harry's launch onto the boat lacked the grace and finesse of the big dogs. He slipped and tumbled, and landed squarely at Grizzly's feet, wriggling like a worm on a hook.

"Watch out for strange looking fish with teeth," Grizzly chuckled. "They might mistake you for food."

"You're the one that ought to watch out for strange looking fish," Harry muttered, picturing Montgomery's underwater fish devices. Then he pictured the grabbing claw and the snapping noises it made.

The claws had sounded like they could crush bone.

"Grizzly..." Harry began.

Grizzly's head snapped around and he gave Harry a dark look. "What now?"

Harry sighed. Grizzly probably wouldn't believe him anyway. "Never mind."

The floor started to move beneath Harry's feet. It took him a moment to realize it was the ferry sluicing through the water.

He peered through an opening in the boat's hull and gave a tentative look toward the shore.

Harry had always believed himself to be a fearless dog. But now he realised the fear he felt must have been similar to what the small dogs experienced whenever they followed him into Big Rover. He only hoped he could face his demons as bravely as his friends had.

As Harry stared at the shore, he saw a large number of cats pushing the fish devices into the water. It was amazing how the cats went undetected by the hundred or more dogs gathered at the shore. Yet the dogs' focus was on the ferry bound for Mystery Island.

Once the fish devices were in the water, the cats pushing them dispersed, leaving that section of the beach empty once more.

A wave hit the starboard side, and the ferry gave a sudden lunge to the left. Harry dug his claws into the deck and closed his eyes.

I can do this, he told himself. What's the worst thing that could happen? Drowning and being eaten by a shark came to mind.

He was starting to feel sick in the stomach.

Harry kept his eyes closed until he noticed the scent that big dogs made when they were excited. Suddenly the air was thick with the smell of custard and salami.

Opening his eyes, the island loomed in front, thick with trees and shadows. The island looked isolated and uninhabited. The awaiting jetty stood silent and alone. Oyster shells clung to the aged footings, so aged that the jetty leaned slightly to the left. Harry expected ghosts to step out from amongst the trees to moor the boat.

"Why did I ever agree to this?" he mumbled to himself. "Swimming is for ducks."

Before Harry could convince himself that,

as a dog, dog-paddling would come naturally to him, the ferry reached the other side. In a fashion much like hounds going after a fox, the big dogs bounded off the boat. Then, madly barking and drooling, they raced to stand in a particular spot on the shore. Harry leapt out of the boat and hurried to do as the other dogs did.

Despite being inches away from the water, he had no time to develop an allergic rash; without warning, a gun went off and the dogs took off.

A diver dives, a belly-flopper belly-flops, and a jumper jumps. Harry entered the water using none of these methods. Rather, he fell in when Chain charged past him. The big dog's gigantic feet knocked Harry over, sending him tumbling down the bank. With a loud *plop* he was neck deep in the water.

Harry kicked and yapped and swallowed mouthfuls of the ocean. The salty water stung his eyes, blinding him. He started to panic. And when he tried to breathe deeply to slow his fast-beating heart, he swallowed another lungful.

"Keep your mouth shut and your head lifted," a Golden Retriever to his left said as she glided by.

"Dog paddling is like running under water," a Border Collie to his right said.

Harry kept his mouth closed and held his head high. He kicked his legs, imagining he was running on the streets of Little Rover.

Dog paddling seemed easy and natural enough, and after a few revolutions, he was swimming.

Although he was going the wrong way.

He continued to swim in circles, until he figured out that if he pulled a little harder with his left legs he could straighten himself up.

Once he was facing in the direction of Buster Bay, he beat his legs like a blender. Instinct told Harry to keep doing what he was doing until he reached the finish line, because if he stopped paddling, he'd surely plunge straight to the bottom and drown.

Chapter 36

A CAT TO THE RESCUE

JUNIOR growled as the four sentinels posted around him and Fleabag's prison flexed their claws. He braced for an attack, then all of a sudden, the cats rushed out of the great chamber.

"Where did they go?" Fleabag asked.

"It doesn't matter. Let's get out of here."

They jumped high into the air, trying to reach the hatch at the top. But the latch for the hatch was too far away.

"Junior, the walls are melting," Fleabag cried out.

He stopped and stared down at his feet. "You're right, Fleabag. Those foolish cats made these contraptions out of ice."

He thumped his paw against the wall. "It's not melting fast enough. The race will be over before it melts."

He and Fleabag continued jumping, but it was no use. The hatch was too high up for them to reach.

As Junior rested to catch his breath, a black cat with yellow eyes scurried across the room. Then it raced up the ladder fixed to the outside and lifted the hatch. With a grin, the cat tossed down a rope.

"I'm Anastasia, a friend of Harry's," the cat said. "Hurry."

Once Junior reached the top of the rope, he glared at the cat. "Why are you helping us?"

"I told you, I'm Harry's friend."

Fleabag, still in the fish device, barked with excitement. "You're the cat in Harry's dreams. You and he met when he was a pup."

Anastasia nodded. "I came to tell Harry to forget about winning this race. My father and I have decided to let the big dogs smash this place apart so we can be free of it." Her ears pricked up. "Hurry, the guards will be back soon. I opened up as many tins of tuna as I could find. But they will soon have eaten them all."

Junior helped Fleabag up the rope. Then the three of them raced across the chamber to the door.

"Oh no," Fleabag cried. "The race is already underway."

"Hurry," Anastasia cried. She bounced from rock to rock with ease. She was halfway down the escarpment before Junior and Fleabag had made it out the door.

The dogs did their best to keep up with the cat. It was when they reached the bottom and took off across the sand that the dogs caught up. Dogs excel at beach sprints. They were by Anastasia's side within seconds. Together, the three of them tore across the sand heading for the jetty. When they reached it, they stood side by side to watch the race.

The dogs were in the water, some of them already halfway across the bay.

"I can't see Harry," Junior said.

Chapter 37

DOGS CAN FLOAT, RIGHT?

HARRY could barely keep his head above water.

The big dogs were already lengths ahead of him. He swam with the frenzy of a goldfish in a pond full of piranha.

All morning he'd been hoping instinct would take over and he'd be able to swim as well as he could run. And while he was doing okay for his first attempt at swimming, he was simply too small to cover any sizeable distance.

So he decided to try another technique.

Harry held his breath and dove beneath the surface. Then he rocked his body back and forth, back and forth, pretending he was a rocking horse. After a few underwater thrusts, the technique seemed to be working.

He was now moving though the water the way a dolphin would.

He was faster than ever. He overtook one big dog. Then he overtook another.

When Harry next dove under the water, however, he was full of elation with his prowess that he forgot to hold his breath.

He broke the surface with water stinging his nostrils. It felt like insects were biting the insides of his nose.

As he snorted out the water, a wave slapped Harry in the face, sending it back down his throat again.

He swallowed a mouthful of salty water, and gagged on it. Then a second wave hit him from behind. It felt like a rock had slammed into him.

Wave after wave assaulted Harry. He realised he was scrambling to grab a hold of the water, which everybody knows is impossible.

His legs were kicking in all directions. Instead of swimming, he was going in circles.

He finally got his legs doing what they were supposed to. But the current was against him. For every thrust forward, the current pushed him back.

The effort was taking its toll on his legs. They felt heavy and useless.

He swallowed another mouthful of water and started to sink.

Harry was drowning.

Chapter 38

SABOTAGE

MONTGOMERY wore a snorkel and goggles inside his underwater fish device. He was pedalling his legs fast to catch up to the big dogs.

"I'll teach those pesky mutts to mess with cats," he said, his voice muffled around the snorkel's mouthpiece.

He switched on his headlights and pedalled toward Grizzly. The big dog was already way out in front. His long legs sliced through the ocean with effortless precision. At the rate Grizzly was swimming, he'd be at the finish line in seconds.

Montgomery pedalled faster.

Then he radioed to the other cats to close in and launch their attack. He was almost close enough to reach out to latch onto Grizzly's legs when the mayday call came in.

"Mayday! Mayday! My fish is cracking up," a muffled voice cried in distress.

"Mine too," said another. "I repeat. Mine too."

"What do you mean your fish are cracking up?" Montgomery asked, clearly annoyed.

Yet, even as he said this, he saw a crack forming in the wall of his fish device. Water trickled through the crack. Slowly at first, like a leaky tap. Drip. Drip. Drip. Then the crack widened enough to poke a blade of grass through.

The flow of water increased. It went from a drip to a *whoosh*. And it whoosh, whoosh, whooshed, until it seemed as though a garden hose had been shoved inside the giant fish bowl.

"You idiot, Montgomery," Humphrey yelled over the radio. "You made these machines out of ice. They're melting in the water."

"It's not as if Cat World has a factory that could make them out of glass," Montgomery replied.

He had used what was on hand, which happened to be an ice machine.

Montgomery watched in horror as the walls of his fish device melted. He saw the other cats , still strapped into their bicycles, sink to the bottom.

Montgomery quickly undid his seatbelt. When his walls fully melted, he swam up to the surface.

Chapter 39

VICTORY CAN WAIT

GRIZZLY was almost at the finish line. With just a few more strokes he'd know the whereabouts of Cat World. Then nothing could stop him from tearing the place apart.

"Victory is mine," Grizzly whooped with satisfaction. "I've got to hand it to you, Harry. You put up one heck of a fight. A more worthy adversary I have yet to meet."

Grizzly turned his head. He had expected to see Harry dog-paddling somewhere near the middle of the pack. He saw the small dog halfway across the bay, all right. But Harry was face down in the water, bobbing along the surface like a buoy.

"Harry!" Grizzly yelled. "Harry! Lift your head up, you stupid mutt. You'll drown if you keep swimming like that."

The small body remained limp. Wave after wave slapped at the small dog.

Grizzly barked once more, this time as loud as a truck horn. But Harry remained floating on the surface.

Yikes, what have I done? Grizzly thought.

"Hang on, buddy," he yelled. "I'm on my way."

Grizzly sped toward the drowning dog. He swam faster than ever, his legs powering through the water, easier now that he was going with the current. Still, he doubled his stride, amazed he had any energy left after swimming almost the entire length of Buster Bay.

Grizzly was a big and powerful dog. He possessed a short temper. And as leader of the big dogs he had a reputation of toughness to uphold. But seeing Harry's lifeless body had sent a shocking revelation through him.

Nothing, not even a statue made out of puppy teeth, was worth the life of a fellow canine.

As Grizzly sailed past Chain and Diesel, Chain said, "You're going the wrong way, boss."

Grizzly ignored him. He pumped his legs through the water. His chest tightened with the pressure of guilt. It would be his fault if the small dog drowned. Competitiveness had made Grizzly dare the small dog to a race in the water. Every dog within a fifty kilometre radius knew about Harry's phobia.

Grizzly was now inches away from the small dog. He barked, sending the seagulls scurrying off. Grizzly grabbed Harry by the collar and yanked his head up out of the water.

He barked in Harry's ear. Still, the small dog was not moving.

Grizzly barked again. Then again and again.

"Come on, Harry," he urged. "Wake up."

At last Harry coughed, spitting up litres of water.

Harry's voice croaked when he said, "Stop barking, Grizzly, or I'm calling the dog rangers on you."

"Thank the bones you're alive," Grizzly said with a gush of relief.

The big dog's heart was still beating wildly, but he dragged Harry by the scruff of his neck across the finish line to the shore, and to safety.

By now the race was over. Diesel had been the first to reach the wooden jetty and he was crowned champion dog-paddler. However, Diesel's victory was short-lived. All the dogs and cats rushed to the shore while Grizzly dragged Harry's sodden body out of the water.

Fleabag and Junior pushed their way through the gathered crowd.

Grizzly let them tend to their friend.

The salty water blurred Grizzly's vision. He would have pounced on anyone who'd said they were tears of joy, but that's exactly what they were.

"Grizzly," Harry's croaked.

Grizzly wandered over.

"You saved my life," Harry said.

"You were drowning."

"Thank you."

"Don't take it as a sign of affection. A drowned dog in Buster Bay is bad for tourism. And tourists are a good source of food scraps."

Harry smiled at Grizzly. "Fleabag was right. You really are a big softie."

Grizzly huffed. "I am not."

Harry was laughing. "Your secret is safe with me."

Grizzly knew this to be true, because Harry had kept his word about not revealing the location of Cat World.

"You're all right, Harry," Grizzly said. Then he added, "For a small dog."

"At least I'm cured of my fear of water," Harry said, standing up and shaking his coat. "But I think I'll leave swimming to the fish."

"Speaking of fish," Fleabag said, "has anybody seen what happened to Montgomery?"

All the dogs turned their heads at that moment to see Montgomery as he emerged from the water. He was dripping with water and wearing the foulest, darkest expression on his face. A large piece of seaweed sat on his head, like a hat.

Montgomery removed the seaweed. Then he pointed a sharp-clawed finger at Harry and Grizzly.

"Because neither of you two is the winner," he shrieked, "all the bets are off. I'll kindly ask you to stay out of cat affairs from now on. You had no right to use Cat World as a wager."

Three more cats dragged themselves out from the water. They spat and hissed, clearly appalled at finding their lush fur coats soaking wet. They gave Montgomery a dark scathing look before they drip, drip, dripped their way to the stormwater drain and disappeared down into the darkness.

Montgomery stayed on the beach. Cats lingered nearby, some near the drain, some on the beach. Grizzly noticed a few cats were gazing up at the sun. As the sun's rays dried his wet coat, he wondered if these cats had ever seen the sun.

Maybe they deserved his pity for being denied the sun, but he couldn't forgive them for turning the puppy teeth into a statue.

"Oohs" and *"ahhs"* cut across the air as an old cat moved through the crowd.

"Cats, cats," he said to those who were staring at the sewer drain. "Stay where you are. You do not have to leave this world until you hear what we have to say."

The old cat turned to face Grizzly. "I am Beauregard. Cat Elder."

More *"oohs"* and *"ahhs"* escaped the crowd. This time caused by Shan and Old Roger strolling up the beach behind Beauregard. It was well known amongst dogs that Shan and Old Roger despised each other. Yet, here they were, acting as though they were the closest of friends.

The crowd parted to let the Elders onto the beach. Many dogs sat down as a sign of respect. Seeing this, most of the other dogs followed suit.

The cats must have taken this as a different meaning, because they began to arch their backs and hiss.

"Silence," Beauregard shouted. He led the way up to the jetty. "It's time to put an end to this nonsense. The dogs want their teeth back. And they shall have them."

"And the cats shall have their freedom," Shan added. "Any cat wishing to return to the surface may do so. No dog will harm them."

This caused a loud meow-like cheer amongst the cats, though their tails swished feverishly. The dogs began to argue amongst themselves.

Was this something that they wanted?

Did they even like cats? Where would the cats live if they were to return to the surface? Surely not amongst the dogs?

Shan glared at the crowd. "No cat will be harmed by a dog. Do you understand?"

Her gaze finally landed on Grizzly's.

"Mum, I love you," the big dog said, "but what they did to our puppy teeth is unforgiveable. They need to be punished."

"At the very least, they owe us an explanation," Harry said.

"The cats owe us nothing," Old Roger sighed. "It is *we* who owe the explanation. We also owe you our sincerest apologies. You see, a long time ago—"

Shan cut him off when she laid a paw on his shoulder. "I'd like to explain, if I may. It seems I owe an explanation to my two dearest friends as well."

She licked Beauregard on the top of his head. She did the same to Old Roger. Then she reached for Grizzly's paw and gave it a gentle squeeze.

He blinked away the salty tears, blaming them yet again on the ocean.

Shan turned to face the old dog and old

cat.

"Please forgive me," she said. "I spoke hurtful words to you both a long, long time ago. Worst of all, I said I never wanted to see you again. And that was wrong."

The crowd sat silent, confused and cynical. Grizzly was even more confused. It was his mother who had told him to search for Cat World.

Shan seemed hesitant to talk at first, but at last she lifted her head high into the air.

"Roger, Beauregard, and I were the best of friends. We'd been abandoned in an alley. A kind butcher took pity on us and fed us sausages. We returned each week for the sausages, even after we'd found homes. To put a long story short, we got greedy, which led to a fight where Roger and I bet the dogs' puppy teeth."

Shan started to cry. Old Roger nudged her gently. Beauregard rubbed his cheek against her leg.

"I'm okay," she sniffled. "I always cry when I get emotional. Anyway, Beauregard only wanted the sausages, but because he was the winner he got to keep the puppy teeth. I am truly sorry, big dogs. It was a stupid thing to do. But that is where the teeth go when you leave them under your pillow."

"I am ashamed of my part in this tale," Old Roger said. "I wish to apologise to the small dogs. And to the Tooth Fairy too, who has been out of business all this time."

Grizzly waited for the old cat to speak.

At last the old cat swished his tail. "They were delicious sausages, but not worth losing two very dear friends. I played a part in the separation of cats and dogs and I am sincerely sorry. It is time to end this feud. It is time for life to return to what it once was, when small dogs, big dogs, and cats lived side by side in harmony."

Beauregard held up a document. "This was drawn up all those years ago. It states that cats are the rightful owners of the puppy teeth. It shows the boundary lines for the three towns, Big Rover, Little Rover, and Cat World. It also contains Dog Law and an inventory of the teeth."

"For the cat's protection," Shan said, "Dog Law was created, and dogs were told that cats were extinct. That is why dogs have to stay inside at night."

Beauregard sighed as he stared up at the sky. "Night time is the only time cats are able to come up to the surface to claim the teeth. It's the only time we are able to breathe fresh air. And because cats can read and write, we held onto this document for safe-keeping. I also held onto three jade stones that, long ago, meant an alliance amongst a cat and two dogs."

The cat held three stones high into the air. Grizzly saw the flash of green against the sunlight. They were pretty stones.

"I would like to pass these stones on to new owners," Beauregard said. "To the three youngsters who have shown great wisdom, compassion, and loyalty over this past week."

He turned to Old Roger and Shan. "May I?"

Shan and Old Roger nodded.

"Harry and Anastasia," said the cat, "I would ask you to please come forward."

The jetty wasn't so big that it could take all the dogs and cats. Grizzly stepped aside to let them on.

Beauregard held up a paw. "You can stay Grizzly. This involves you too."

"Me?" Grizzly said, alarmed. "I didn't do anything. You can't pin this on me."

Shan chuckled. "No, Grizzly. He means that you saved Harry's life. You put friendship above winning. I know I told you to win at all costs, but that was wrong of me. You showed good leadership skills today."

"That's right," Beauregard said. "Grizzly, Harry, and Anastasia, please accept these stones and guide the next generation of cats and dogs into a new era."

Cheers erupted amongst the cats and dogs. Grizzly couldn't stop the smile from spreading across his face as he accepted the jade stone.

When the cheers died down, a series of boos and hisses issued from down near the beach.

"Oh, boo hoo," Montgomery said.

He strode up toward the jetty, shaking sand out of his fur. His features were twisted in anger. It caused a growl to bubble inside Grizzly's throat.

"So you three had a lover's tiff," Montgomery said. "And now you're old and dying, and you want to beg forgiveness from each other. In the meantime, we have a perfectly functioning system amongst cats and dogs. Why ruin a good thing?"

"Because cats want to be free, Montgomery," Anastasia said. She stood by Harry's side and held tightly onto his paw. "Cats and dogs are free to live together in harmony once again."

Montgomery addressed the cats that had remained on the beach. "Dogs love rules and routine. If you live with them, you'll have to abide by these rules and routines. Is that what you want?"

Old Roger lifted himself up onto the box of tinned dog food to be awarded to the winner.

"Many of these rules exist for the protection of cats too," he told the cats. "The rest of Dog Law is there to stop dogs doing stupid things."

Montgomery waved his paw. "You'll simply make up new rules." He crossed his paws over his chest. "I will never do as a dog says."

"You are free to return to Cat World and live there if you wish," Beauregard said. "In fact, any cat wishing to remain in Cat World is free to do so. But never let it be said that you were forced to stay. A new era has come for cats and dogs."

A cheer went up amongst every cat and dog.

Montgomery hissed and spat and he trudged his way to the stormwater drain. He gave Grizzly, Harry, and Anastasia a lingering dark stare, then he vanished into Cat World.

A large number of cats glanced up at the jetty. Then they glanced down at the drain Montgomery had fled down into. As if trying to decide what they wanted.

Finally, and to Grizzly's pleasure, many of these cats followed Montgomery down the sewer.

"There's still the issue of the statue," Grizzly said to Anastasia.

Anastasia flicked her tail in the air. "I agree, it is hideous."

"Let's smash it," Grizzly said with a grin.

Harry held up a paw. "It must be *dismantled*. Not smashed. These are our puppy teeth, Grizzly."

"Yes, you're right. It just makes me so angry to think about it."

"It was anger that caused this fiasco in the

first place," Harry said.

Grizzly scowled at the small dog. "Just don't make me regret saving your life."

***

DOGS AND CATS from Little Rover, Big Rover, and Cat World helped with dismantling the puppy teeth statue. Except for Montgomery and the cats who vowed to have nothing to do with this treaty, of course. They played ping-pong and sang on the Karaoke machine.

It took a few days to dismantle the statue, and another few days to hand the teeth back to their rightful owners. Or to their rightful owner's descendants in some cases. Those cats who wished to return to the surface were given guided tours around Dog Town to find suitable housing.

Some dogs grew impatient with the cats, who had an unbridled fussiness about beds and food bowls. After two days, these dogs told the cats to look for their own homes.

Other dogs quickly embraced the idea that cats now lived amongst them. In their haste to be loved, the dogs shared their toys, their food bowls, their beds, and their yards. Pretty soon the dogs became fed up with the cats, who possessed an unbridled self-centredness about which toys were theirs.

Thus the dogs invented a new set of rules, titled Property Law.

After a week, a group of small dogs and big dogs demanded that Harry and Grizzly do something about removing the pesky cats from Dog Town.

At the same time, cats demanded Anastasia do something about the dogs leaving their potty all over the yard.

Of course, neither of these new leaders could do anything about the squabbles, because of the three jade stones that represented the new alliance.

The cats and dogs would need to work hard at living together and sharing houses, beds, food, and playthings.

Eventually they did.

It was somewhat harmonious.

Chapter 40

NEW BEGINNINGS

HARRY pressed the remote control. "Hurry up Montgomery, it's starting."

Montgomery entered the room carrying a large bowl of popcorn. "Don't I get a say in what we watch on TV?"

His face was screwed up like he'd smelled something awful. Harry realized that was just the way the cat normally looked. He'd gotten used to it. Just like he'd gotten used to visiting Cat World with his best friends, Junior and

Fleabag. The three of them were now seated on the comfy sofa in front of the TV.

"I'd prefer it if we watched Garfield instead of Underdog," Montgomery said, putting the bowl of popcorn on the table and squeezing in between Fleabag and Junior. "Or better yet, how about I watch Garfield and you three go back to Dog Town?"

"Are you trying to get rid of us already?" Junior asked. "We've grown accustomed to this place."

Harry wriggled his toes in the foot-spa. "Yes, we rather like coming down here for a visit."

He was pleased at how he'd overcome his fear of water. He was pleased with much of what he'd accomplished. He'd rescued a bunch of cats from a vengeful big dog. He had unknowingly played a part in reconciling three old friends. He had retrieved their puppy teeth. More importantly, he had learned the truth about cats and dogs.

Fleabeag reached over and scooped a pawful of popcorn into her mouth. Then she gulped it down without chewing, the way dogs do.

"We like Cat World now that the statue's been dismantled and our teeth returned," she said. "Cat World has a unique ambience."

"How lucky for me," Montgomery muttered.

"Can we still call this place Cat World now that is no longer filled with cats?" Junior asked.

Montgomery glared at him. "Forget about any name changes. This place is, and will always be, Cat World."

"Junior has a point," Harry said. "Perhaps we should think up some new names for the towns. What about Upper Dog Town and Lower Dog Town?"

Montgomery flicked his tail, clearly not amused. "I still have a lot of influence amongst the cats. If you wretched dogs make plans to change the name of Cat World, I will see to it that you are stopped."

"Are you always this grouchy?" Fleabag asked.

Montgomery smiled. "Yes, but you know what cheers me up? A sing-along. Here, let me crank up the karaoke machine."

"Noooo!" the dogs shouted in unison.

"Dogs are no fun," Montgomery said, then

he headed off into another room.

Harry nestled his backside into the sofa. Cat World indeed had *ambience*, as Fleabag put it, yet it was missing one key ingredient.

Anastasia was gone.

Harry let out a sigh. "I do hope Anastasia is all right. I still can't believe she decided to hand the jade stone to Montgomery so she could travel the world."

"Read the note again," Fleabag said.

The cats were teaching the dogs to read. This was another of Harry's accomplishments that he was pleased about. He'd excelled in his reading lessons.

He unfolded the letter:

Dearest Harry,

You saved us. You saved *me*. And now that I am free, I cannot live in that dreary chamber and become a leader. I want to travel the world. I yearn to feel the sunlight on my back. I can smell the faraway oceans, and I want to see them.

That is why I have handed my jade stone to

Montgomery. He was always a leader, maybe not a very good one, but he did take care of us. He needs to learn how to live with dogs and be kind to everyone. And with your guidance, he can master both things.

Please take care of yourself until I return.
Anastasia

"She'll be back," Junior said. "And when she returns, think of all the wonderful tales she'll have to tell us."

Harry nodded. "Yes, think of all those wonderful tales."

"In the meantime, you need to prepare for the next Dog Paddle Challenge. It is only two-hundred and sixty days away."

Harry pulled his paws out of the spa.

"Yikes. No thanks. That's one Dog Law rule I don't want to change."

Okay, so maybe he wasn't completely over his fear of water.

All in good time, he told himself. All in good time.

THE END

DOG LAW

Big dogs live in Big Rover. Small dogs live in Little Rover.

Small dogs are forbidden from entering the Dog Paddle Challenge.

Big dogs and small dogs shall NOT mingle, except during the Dog Paddle Challenge, when all dogs may congregate on the beach to watch.

Younger pups must follow their elder siblings wherever they go.

All dogs are to remain off the streets at night.

Dogs must always tell the truth.

Betting is forbidden - dares are permitted.

Giant snakes with three heads live in the forest. Small dogs are prohibited from entering this forest.

Never rush the potty. This leads to complications and unwanted trips to the vet.

Obey rules one to nine and everything else is worth getting into trouble for.

PROPERTY LAW

If it's in my mouth, it's mine.

If you drop it, it's mine.

If it's in my bowl, it's mine.

If it's not yours, it's mine.

If I find it, it's mine.

If you lose it, it's mine.

If I lick it, it's mine.

If I leave it somewhere, it's still mine.

If it fits in my mouth, it's mine.

If it's broken, it's yours.

About the author

Debbie L Richardson was born in Dublin, Ireland and grew up in Australia. It was always crowded and noisy in the family home. At one stage there were three dogs, a cat, a budgie, and three mice living with seven people in the same house.

Debbie learned to find a quiet space within books.

She now lives on the south coast of New South Wales, Australia with her husband and a small dog named Teeka.

You may learn more about her other fiction novels, published as D L Richardson, at her author website:

www.dlrichardson.com

The Cast of Dog Town

"Dog Town" is an adventure story, filled with wonderful animal characters. Suitable for fans of "Wind in the Willows" and "Watership Down".

With its anthropomorphised characters, "Dog Town" is an ideal book for parents, teachers, or students to read out loud in class, on stage, or at home. Let yourself and others transform into these characters and make their voices heard.

The Small Dogs

HARRY	Brown dog
JUNIOR	Beagle
FLEABAG	Chihuahua
OLD ROGER	Miniature Fox Terrier

The Big Dogs

GRIZZLY	Doberman Pincer
SHAN	Great Dane

The Cats

ANASTASIA	Black cat
MONTGOMERY	Persian
BEAUREGARD	Grey tabby cat

Narrator

NARRATOR	Who do you think this is? A bird? A possum?

Read on for the list of chapters...

The Small Dogs

HARRY   Chapters: 1, 2, 3, 6, 7, 8, 10, 11, 16, 18, 19, 22, 24, 26, 29, 35, 37, 40

JUNIOR   Chapters: 4, 5, 12, 13, 36

FLEABAG   Chapter: 9

OLD ROGER Chapters: 17, 30, 32

The Big Dogs

GRIZZLY   Chapters: 6, 14, 19, 23, 39

SHAN   Chapter: 33

The Cats

ANASTASIA   Chapters: 11, 20, 28

MONTGOMERY   Chapters: 21, 25, 27, 29, 38

BEAUREGARD   Chapters: 15, 32

Narrator

NARRATOR Chapters: 3, 25, 26, 34, 39, Dog Law, Property Law

Printed in Great Britain
by Amazon

59348568R00158